ARTIST POINT

A Sweet National Parks Romance

JULIE MILO

www.juliemilo.com

Cover Design by Sydney Christensen Creations

ISBN: 9798991947183

For the author of all the beauty in all the world.
Perfection is His alone.

"God gave us eyes to see the beauty in nature and hearts to see the beauty in each other."

Author's Note

This romance novel is meant to be a sweet escape. However, it does contain some themes that readers may want to be aware of before deciding to read it. Be aware if you keep reading this note, there are some spoilers.

This book contains no sex on the page, no swearing, and no deaths (animal or human). This book contains:

- A parent's death from cancer (in the past),
- A parent betraying their adult child,
- A medical emergency (off page) with scenes taking place in the hospital, including discussions of injuries.

Chapter One

Taylor

"Look around the room." George, the owner of Bear and Bison Ranch nods his cowboy-hatted head and twitches his gray mustache. "The people you see here will be your best friends by the end of orientation and your family by the end of the summer."

Obediently, I turn in my seat to look at the other fifteen or so men and women in their early twenties who will also be working at B&B Ranch—a vacation guest ranch in northwest Wyoming outside of Cody.

I spot Becca, my roommate, near the back of the group. We met briefly this afternoon while I was unpacking in our cabin. Hers is the only familiar face in the bunch.

As I shift my shoulders to face the front again, my eyes snag on another of my new coworkers. He's lean, his oversized hooded sweatshirt creating a bulk around him that's obviously false. He has a blue ball cap pulled low across his forehead, shadowing his eyes under the artificial light of the lodge dining room. Ordinary height—from what I can tell while he's sitting down—and most of his features are obscured between the hoodie and the cap. It's the ball cap that catches my attention. Most of the men here, and many of the women, too, are wearing cowboy hats. We're on a ranch in Wyoming after all.

George's voice sounds again from the front of the room and reminds me to face forward. Before I can move, the man with the ball cap lifts his head and catches me looking. I see a flash of his brown eyes and his lips turning up in a smile before I spin around, my face warming.

He's handsome, I think, then scold myself for once again acting like an awkward preteen in front of a cute guy. It's pretty much my MO.

I focus my attention on George, who's telling us what needs to be done around the ranch in the next couple of weeks ahead of the first guests arriving.

I'm surprised to hear there are no horses yet. They don't stay on the ranch year-round. No one does, since it's too remote to live safely in the snowy winters.

A nearby working ranch rents the horses to B&B for the summers, and they'll be bringing a group over later in the week for me and the other wranglers to start working with. We'll need to learn their personalities and quirks so we can match them with guests and each other—pairing the gentlest animals with children and knowing which horses get along and which don't.

After running through an exhausting list of chores, George introduces his wife and the co-owner of B&B Ranch, Pamela.

While George is tall and wiry, Pamela is short and round. Her long gray hair is braided down her back, swishing across the fabric of her paisley Western shirt as she speaks, her head tilting as she scans the crowd.

Pamela smiles brightly. "Who's ready for the summer of a lifetime?" She whoops and pumps her fist.

We all clap and cheer, whistling and stomping our feet.

I notice quickly that George is all business, and Pamela is clearly in charge of enthusiasm. He smiles softly at her as she winds us up.

When the noise finally dies down, Pamela continues. "One of your first tasks will be to make a name tag for yourself. Our goal today is for everyone to get to know each other and B&B so that tomorrow we can launch into the more manual labor of preparing the ranch.

"Not any old 'Hi, my name is' name tag, though. We have materials set up on the table, and your assignment is to make a name tag that represents who you are. How do you want to introduce yourself to the family you'll be with for the next three months?"

I peer at the table with the supplies and consider how to make my name tag represent who I am. My interests are simple: family, beauty, and horses. All three are tied in some way to why I'm in Wyoming this summer, across the country from everything I know.

Earlier this month, I graduated from college. I majored in art because that's what I love, and I didn't give any thought to employability because, frankly, I expected I'd be getting my "MRS degree" along with my BFA. Not that I had a mister lined up; I assumed it would be easy to meet the love of my life from the thousands of men at the large state university less than an hour from my hometown.

Spoiler alert: It was not.

As my senior year wound down with lots of first and second dates that amounted to nothing, I started to panic. It was in that state of panic that I applied for a dozen equestrian-related jobs, including the one here at B&B, in that nebulous week between Christmas and New Year's when I never really know what day it is or when I last ate anything that wasn't cheese or chocolate.

It's not that I think I need a man to take care of me. It's that all I've dreamed of my whole life is being a wife and mother. I know I have skills I can use to earn money, but nothing sounds nicer to me than spending my days on a modest piece of land somewhere loving my husband, raising our kids, and creating my art without the pressure of commercialism.

That's not how it worked out for me, though. My parents warned me; my friends warned me. I learned the hard way, keeping my head in the clouds too long, and now I need to reimagine a future for myself after Plan A didn't go at all how I thought it would.

Now, I'm not panicked anymore like I was at Christmas. I've put it out of my mind and am focusing on this summer—the new, exciting experiences I'll have as part of this Wyoming adventure. Everything else will work itself out eventually.

I shake the thoughts from my head. *Name tag*. I join my coworkers at the table and find the acrylic tag about the size of a playing card that has my name on it. I snag several paint pens in bright colors to take back to my table.

I start by drawing colorful wildflowers around the edges: yellow, purple, red, and pink. Along the bottom, I add a buckskin Paso Fino horse like my sweet Serena back home, nibbling at the blossoms. I smile to myself, feeling suddenly homesick even though it was only yesterday that I took Serena for a farewell-for-now ride at my parents' horse farm. It's the distance, I think, more so than the time away that has me in my feelings.

Pamela claps her hands. "When you finish, find a partner and share how your name tag represents you."

I put the finishing touches on my piece and stand to search for a partner when a throat clears behind me.

It's the guy wearing the ball cap. My heart stutters as I wonder at him crossing the room to approach *me*.

"Hey," he says.

I tilt my head to the side, taking in the details of his face I couldn't see from across the room earlier. Thick, dark eyebrows, long eyelashes, wavy wisps of golden-brown hair poking out from beneath the cap, thin lips turned up in a smile, and the smallest dimple on his right cheek. He really is handsome.

"Hey."

"I love your name tag." He leans over the table, studying the paint that's still drying. Standing straight again, he meets my eyes. "Taylor."

I'm suddenly too warm. The back of my neck prickles, and I look away. "Um, thanks."

He sticks out his hand. "I'm Jackson."

Still flushed, I grab his hand and shake. "I'm Taylor." His warm eyes twinkle, and I realize my mistake. "Oh, right, you already knew that. Sorry."

I wipe my palms against my jeans. *Can you behave like a normal human for even a second, Tay?*

Jackson chuckles. He gestures toward my name tag and folds his arms over his chest. Lowering his chin, he grins at me. "I'll show you mine if you show me yours."

His teasing words are so unexpected that a short bark of laughter bursts out of me. In trying to rein it back in, I snort.

Jackson's grin widens. The line could have been creepy or annoying coming from a different man, but something about the boyish ease in his expression relaxes me.

I nudge his sneaker with the toe of my boot. "You first."

He extends his arm and opens his hand to display a tag with his name in the center. To the right is the outline of two hastily drawn mountain peaks that reach from the bottom edge to the top. Fluffy clouds fill the rest of the space.

I tip my chin up in question.

"My two loves," he explains. "The mountains and the sky."

I wait for him to continue. "I'm an aeronautical engineer and hobby pilot. The first of those being how I pay the bills. The bills in question, though, are mostly tied to my real passion: mountain climbing."

I lean back, my eyes widening. "Impressive and intriguing." I tap my chin. "I have so many questions."

His cheeks turn pink. "Tell me about your name tag first."

I pick it up from the table and hold it out so he can see it better. "I'm an artist, first and foremost. I love finding beauty in the world. The obvious things like flowers and trees and snowcapped mountains, but the hidden beauty, too." I trace the tip of my finger over the subtle texture I've painted on the flower petals. "A ripple on the water. The perfect spiral inside a seashell. I notice details."

Jackson stills, and I raise my eyes to find him watching me, unblinking. His lips part. I'm still trying to decode his reaction when it's gone. In one flurry of movement, he snaps his mouth closed and shifts his eyes back to our name tags.

"And the horse?"

I giggle, pushing away my curiosity at Jackson's reaction. "That one's obvious. I'm here as a 'wrangler.' I grew up on my parents' horse farm in Ocala, Florida, where they breed and train thoroughbreds."

He lifts his eyebrows. "Florida, huh? You're a long way from home."

"Yep." I don't tell him that this summer will be my first time ever living outside of Florida. I've vacationed up and down the East Coast, but I've never been this far west before.

"What about you?" I volley back. "Where are you from?" And why is he working a summer job at a guest ranch if he's an aeronautical engineer? And does he really climb mountains and fly airplanes for fun?

"Colorado. The Boulder area."

"And what brings you to B&B Ranch this summer?"

He starts to answer, but George is back in the front of the room calling us all to attention. Jackson murmurs a quiet "Nice to meet you," and returns to his seat across the room.

I watch him go, already feeling the first shivers of a crush roll across my shoulders. I tell myself it's just curiosity—he's handsome, with interesting hobbies and a friendly smile. Why wouldn't I want to know more? It doesn't mean I'm going to fall for him.

And anyway, he'll probably run screaming the minute he knows I'm only interested in a real relationship with the potential for a future. It's what they all do.

Chapter Two

Jackson

As George drones on at the front of the room—the same details I've heard him repeat for four summers now—my eyes keep wandering to Taylor's bouncing ponytail of caramel-brown hair.

There's something about her. It's not her looks, though she's beautiful in that innocent, girl-next-door way. Lots of the women in the room tonight are attractive. Many of them I know from past summers, their presence welcome and familiar the way it is with old friends.

George wasn't kidding that the experience of working together at B&B Ranch all summer bonds us together like family. There's not much choice but to get along. The nearest town, Cody, is almost an hour's drive away. Cell phones don't work out here, and the lack of Wi-Fi is part of the intentional charm of a stay at B&B. There's an old desktop computer in the lodge library that's hooked up to satellite internet, but it's for everyone—staff and guests alike—to share, most useful for checking flight information or sending a quick email.

Even on my days off, I'm more likely to head even farther away from civilization than into it, so the people here at B&B are *my* people in a way I'm lacking in other spaces in my life.

That's part of it, maybe. Taylor is new. As one of the old hands on the ranch, a step below management, really, I feel responsible for seeking out the newcomers and making them feel included and welcome.

But I also can't get something she said out of my mind.

Seashells.

The perfect spiral inside seashells, a visual representation of the Fibonacci sequence and its ideal mathematical harmony. The golden ratio. Perfection. We use it in our calculations for fluid dynamics in turbine blade design. It reduces drag, minimizes turbulence.

I always think of seashells when I think of the golden ratio, but it's not often that it happens the other way around. Seashells are not a topic that come up often in Colorado or Wyoming, in the office or the production hangar or on the tops of mountains. The places where I spend the majority of my time.

So, usually my thought pattern goes from turbines to the golden ratio to seashells to my mother.

Skipping right to the end of that sequence when Taylor mentioned seashells was jarring. Immediately, images of my mother in her greenhouse, surrounded by flowers and the seashells she'd collected over years of beach vacations, sprang to mind. It's where she felt most like herself, where I would find her when I got home from school, even though she was supposed to be resting. My mother's greenhouse is where she looked most whole, most strong and healthy, even on her bad days.

"There's beauty everywhere around us, Jackson. You just have to open your eyes."

A sudden din around me dissipates her voice and brings me back to the present. My coworkers scuff chairs across the floor as they stand. I blink, aware that either I've missed the instructions for a new activity, or we've been dismissed for the night.

Some folks head out of the lodge, likely bound for the quiet of their cabins, and some move into the saloon for pickup games of pool or checkers.

The staff at B&B fall into five primary categories: owners and managers, kitchen staff, wranglers, activity guides, and cabin wranglers.

Activity guides like me are responsible for any non-horse guest activities on the ranch: fly-fishing on the Shoshone River, archery, tours of Yellowstone National Park, and more.

Cabin wrangler is B&B's fancy name for housekeepers. They clean the guest cabins and the lodge each day, with a deep clean on the weekends between groups.

The wranglers are the staff with expertise in horses, like Taylor. I was surprised to learn she's a wrangler because George and Pamela rarely allow new staff in that role. Generally, you start as a cabin wrangler your first summer and learn about the horses if you want to return as a wrangler the following year. Taylor must have serious experience with horses if she's brand new and a wrangler. She did say she grew up on a horse farm.

I get my roommate's attention across the room. Nick and I worked and roomed together the previous two summers. He's a good friend I keep up with the rest of the year, too. He lives and goes to school in North Carolina where he's getting a business degree.

Gesturing toward the door with my head, I let him know I'm heading out. In response, he jerks his thumb behind him to the saloon to let me know he's going to play a couple of rounds of pool before calling it a night.

Pamela catches me on the front porch of the lodge as I'm about to make my escape down the stairs.

"Jackson!" she calls.

I put on my happy face and turn around. "Hey, Pamela! It's great to be back for another summer."

"And we are so glad you are! You're always such a bright spot, and the guests love you, especially the kids. It's so good to see you."

She tucks me into a hug, and I tense. Part of me wants to sink into her motherly arms, but a bigger part warns me to keep my distance, that comfort doesn't last for long.

I pat her twice on the back, and she lets go.

"Oh, sorry. I forgot you aren't a hugger."

I smile. "That's okay. I'm pretty beat, though. I need to get my rest for a long day of George's chores tomorrow!"

She laughs, deep and from her belly. "You do that. I'll see you in the morning."

"Good night." I shoot her a half wave as she goes back into the lodge.

I'm free now to walk back to my cabin, but I'm feeling restless and introspective, so instead I continue down the path toward the pole barn. The sun is starting to set behind the mountains, creating a pink glow in the sky.

Getting outside under the big, open sky with the mountains on the horizon always helps to settle me so I can process my thoughts and emotions better. So does walking.

I pass in front of several guest cabins, dark and quiet now, but before long they'll be filled with sounds of life. Kids cranky after a full day of doing things they've never done before, overtired but refusing to sleep. Couples lounging on their front porches, talking and laughing, reconnecting, looking at each other instead of tiny screens in their hands.

Families connecting in a way I miss so badly my chest aches.

Past the cabins, I come to a wooden footbridge that crosses over Libby Creek. I stop in the middle of the bridge and lean my forearms against the top of the railing, leaning over to peer into the water below. I close my eyes and let the sound of the clear water bubbling over the rocks soothe me.

After a few quiet moments, I open my eyes and continue to the pole barn in an attempt to find her there, feel my mother's presence in a place she would have loved.

Like the guest cabins, the pole barn and corral are empty for now, which is how I like them best. In a couple of days, the pasture will be teeming with horses. I'll help when needed, but after the horses arrive, I try to avoid this part of the ranch as much as possible.

I lean against the post-and-board fence that surrounds the corral. Again, my mother's voice echoes in my ears, telling me it's okay to be afraid and it's brave to try.

I'm so like her in some ways and so different in others. She loved horses, for one, and I can't stand them. But she was a risk-taker, too, in ways that seem far more dangerous to me than flying a plane thousands of feet off the ground or hanging on sheets of ice high on a mountain with two metal handles and some spikes on my boots holding me in place.

Mine are calculated risks. My knowledge of physics reassures me that each cause will have a known effect that I can predict, or even control in the right circumstances. Her risks, though—the trust she put in people—terrifies me. People are unpredictable. Much like horses.

I don't like feeling like this: morose and reclusive. Especially on my first day at the ranch. B&B is my happy place. Well, the one happy place I have that doesn't involve putting my life in jeopardy.

I trace my gloomy mood back to Taylor, back to her saying "seashells" and making me think about my mother.

The phone call I had with my dad right before leaving Cody for the ranch this morning isn't helping my disposition either. Speaking of people who can't be trusted.

Every so often he gets these ideas for get-rich-quick schemes that require more start-up funds than he has on hand. He thinks that because I have an impressive job, I must have money to burn, and that I'd be happy to "loan" it to him.

No matter how many times I've refused, he doesn't stop asking.

I shift away from the fence and start walking the long way back to my cabin.

Nick greets me at the door with a teasing smile. "Where were you? I played two games of pool and still beat you back to the cabin."

I do my best to echo his energy. "Walking around. I missed this place."

Though I try to keep my tone light, he must hear something in it. His eyes narrow in concern as he studies my face. "You okay, man?"

I wave a hand. "Yeah, I'm good."

"You sure?" His brow furrows.

Am I? Nick's one of the few people who knows how I lost my mother and about the problems I have with my dad—the *only* person at the ranch who knows. I could tell him I'm struggling tonight, that the grief flooded me out of nowhere and is threatening to drown me. He would understand.

But no. I can handle it on my own.

I nod and smile. "I'm sure."

Get it together, I tell myself. Tomorrow I'll be back on my game. I'll be the bright and cheery Jackson George and Pamela are expecting this summer. I'll stop dwelling on these thoughts bringing me down. And I'll look at Taylor like she's any other coworker, find some way to keep her and her seashells out of my head.

Chapter Three

Taylor

AS EAGER AS I am to get to know my new coworkers after George releases us from orientation, the headache forming behind my eyes reminds me that I've been up since five this morning and had a full first day on the ranch.

I had trouble sleeping in the lonely hotel room in Cody I stayed in last night, and the time difference between here and home doesn't help.

Yesterday was an all-day journey from home to Wyoming that included a lengthy layover in Denver before I boarded a puddle jumper for the last short leg of the trip. Okay, not exactly a puddle jumper, but the plane was tiny—two seats on each side of a narrow aisle. And the turbulence about took me out. When I was on solid ground again in the Cody airport, I wanted to kiss it.

I stifle a yawn as I bumble down the lodge's front porch stairs to the dirt path that will take me up the hill to my cabin.

"Taylor, wait up!"

My roommate, Becca, is jogging after me. "Are you turning in, too?" she asks.

"Yup. I'm exhausted."

"Same."

It's not a long walk to the cabin, but it's the first chance Becca and I have had to get to know each other today.

By the time we reach our heavy wooden door, I've learned that Becca is from Texas and this is her second summer working at B&B. Like most of the staff, she's in college, heading into her senior year at Texas A&M in the fall.

"Are a lot of the other staff returners, too?" I ask.

She considers, scrunching up her forehead. "About half, maybe? There's always George and Pamela, of course, and Dennis and Leanne are the managers. Dennis is in charge of the activity guides, and Leanne is our supervisor for the horse activities. The lead wrangler. They're married and live year-round in Cody."

Dennis and Leanne look to be a decade or so older than the other staff. It makes sense that they're full-time employees of the ranch, versus me and the other "wranglers" being temporary and seasonal.

"And then there's Chip," Becca continues. "He's the cook. Lisa is his assistant. They're more permanent employees, too. But everyone else is like us: here for the summer. Of that group, five of us worked at B&B last summer. Me, Ashley, Sam, Nick, and Jackson."

Jackson. At the mention of his name, my heartbeat speeds up.

"What's his deal?" I ask, careful to keep my voice even. "Jackson, I mean. He paired up with me for the name tag activity."

Becca nods. "That sounds like Jackson. He's a super friendly, really nice guy. Considers himself to be sort of an unofficial ambassador for the ranch. He's a temporary summer employee like us, but he's a little older.

I think twenty-four? He started working summers here in college and didn't want to stop even after he graduated and started his career back in Colorado. He's got some sort of job that gives him summers off."

"He said he's an aeronautical engineer?"

"Yeah, he designs and builds airplanes. But his real passion is climbing. Last summer, he was always disappearing on his days off, I assume to climb, but he didn't talk about himself much."

"He said something tonight about rock climbing."

She shrugs. "Yeah, you'll have to ask him about it, though. He hasn't shared the details."

As I change into my pajamas and brush my teeth, I marvel at the idea of mountain climbing as a hobby. Florida doesn't even have mountains.

The whole ride to the ranch from Cody this morning, I couldn't tear my eyes away from the scenery outside the van window. We drove through a tunnel and came out to walls of white rocks looming over clear water. As we continued up the mountain, the rock formations and mountain peaks surrounded us. No flat land or swamps here.

Even at the ranch, the mountains seem to scream up into the sky, jagged and foreboding, but also majestic. I can't imagine climbing one. Like all the way to the top? Where the trees thin out into rocks and snow? I shudder, imagining the danger. *No, thank you.*

WE'RE UP EARLY THE next morning. Breakfast is in the lodge at seven, and then we've got chores all day to get ready for the horses to arrive tomorrow.

I shower and pull on jeans and a long-sleeve, button-up Carhartt shirt. I tie my still-damp hair into a ponytail on top of my head and slip my feet into my worn leather boots.

As I wait for Becca, I step out onto the small front porch framed with log banisters. And then I step immediately back into the cabin to retrieve my flannel-lined jacket. I'm not used to being cold in May, that's for sure. I slip my phone from my pocket to check the temperature, but with no data service, the weather app won't update.

Now appropriately bundled, I step back onto the porch and quickly open the camera on my phone.

Because there, in front of my cabin in an open grassy area, is a buffalo. His head is bent low as he grazes on grass and wildflowers. Thick, shaggy fur covers his shoulders and back, though his rump is bare from where he's already shed his winter coat. Pointed gray horns stick out from either side of his fluffy head.

I giggle as I remember the tongue-in-cheek warning I saw printed on T-shirts in an airport shop in Cody: "Don't pet the fluffy cows!"

Now, with a fluffy cow in front of me, I understand the temptation, but I also have enough respect for the power of these animals that I would never give into it.

I do take a video and snap some more pictures, though.

He sets quite the picturesque tableau, my buffalo. Behind him, evergreen trees poke up from the hills into the gray sky. Beyond that, the rugged, snowcapped mountains loom.

Becca gasps quietly as she comes out of the cabin and stands next to me. "So cool!" she whispers. "They make their way to the ranch every now and again. You know, while George and Pamela own the buildings here on the ranch, this is public land. Yellowstone is down the road, and of course the animals can't tell where the national park ends."

"What do we do?" I whisper back. "Wait here until he moves?"

"No. That could take ages. We can walk around him if we keep our distance. He probably has friends nearby somewhere, too, so let's be careful."

I nod, but before I can work up the nerve to move from the safety of the porch to the gravel pathway that leads past the buffalo to the lodge, the door of the cabin next to ours creaks open.

I do a double take when I see Jackson shuffle outside, another man close behind him. My breath catches—another sign that I'm developing a crush on Jackson already—and I quickly give myself a mental scolding.

I've had intense crushes, especially when I was in high school and early on in college. I would start planning ways to run into the guy, like riding my bike the long way home from school so I could pass his house or studying in the library at a certain time when I knew he tended to be there, too. They became all-encompassing to the point of being almost . . . creepy.

No wonder they had never panned out.

Still, the last time I got *that* hung up on a guy was more than three years ago. I'd like to think I've matured since then. Maybe gotten less awkward. Just because I find a man to be handsome and sweet and interesting doesn't mean I need to let him take over my whole existence. I tried that route, and I'm still single, so it's obviously time for a new strategy, like focusing on myself and my happiness rather than getting some man's attention.

Anyway, I guess Jackson and I are neighbors. But it's fine. It'll be fine.

"Pretty cool, huh?" Jackson calls over to us. They join us on our porch, and Jackson's roommate introduces himself as Nick.

I nod, my eyes still fixed on the beast in front of us. "I've never seen a buffalo in the wild before."

Jackson sucks a breath in through his teeth and grins. "Don't let George hear you call it that. That is an American bison, ma'am. Not a buffalo."

I squint toward the buff—I mean, bison—and then at Jackson. "What's the difference?"

Jackson affects a gruff, deep voice meant to imitate George's old cowboy twang. "Well, young lady, you see it's all about the three *H*'s: home, hump, and horn."

Becca snorts. "That sounds like the start of a bad joke."

Jackson's grin widens, and he holds up a finger. When he speaks again, it's in his normal voice. "Home. Buffalo only live in Asia and Africa, while bison are in North America and Europe." He ticks up another finger. "Hump. Bison have large humps at their shoulders, but buffalo do not." Lifting a third finger, he continues. "And horn. Buffalo horns are huge, not like these short daggers on our bison friend here."

I scrunch up my face. "But what about the song?"

Jackson frowns. "What song?"

From behind him, Nick sings hilariously off-key. "Ohhh, give me a home, where the buffalo roam . . ."

"Oh, yeah. That song."

"Yeah, that song. So, why does the song say 'buffalo'?"

"Confused explorers probably." Jackson shrugs. "But because of that song, people pretty much use the two terms interchangeably when they're talking about our fluffy cow friends. Just don't let George hear you say it." He winks.

A loud clanging noise coming from the direction of the lodge makes me jump. Becca laughs. "It's the meal bell," she explains. "We ring it before every meal. When guests are here, we let the kids do it."

Nick jerks his thumb toward the lodge. "We better get going to breakfast."

The bell must have startled the bison, too, because he's lumbering farther up the hill away from us.

We take the opportunity to race down the path toward the lodge.

Chapter Four

Jackson

AFTER BREAKFAST, WE SPEND most of the day getting the pole barn and corrals ready for the horses: pitching hay, checking the fence line, and inspecting the saddles and other tack that have been sitting in storage since last summer.

I help unload bales of hay from the truck, and then Nick and I walk the fence together. We find a few places that need repair, so we pull off the rotted planks and replace them with new ones. We talk as we work.

"Are you excited for your senior year?" I ask Nick.

He nods, unzipping his fleece jacket. The weather isn't quite giving off summer vibes yet—though the high is supposed to get above sixty today—but the sky is clear and the sun heats us in a way that starts like a warm flame against our skin and then seeps inward.

"Yeah. It's my last summer here, though. By this time next year, I'll have a job with all the other chumps in the real world." He tips his head toward me, his lips turned up at the corners. "Although you've managed to avoid it pretty well so far."

I snort, using the claw on my hammer to pry out the nails connecting a splintered slat of wood to the fence post. "Avoid the real world? I wish."

"Well, you're here again this summer, aren't you?"

I look up at the mountain peaks that dominate the skyline from the ranch. My heart starts racing in a spike of adrenaline as I remember scaling those peaks. Well, maybe not exactly those, but I've conquered most of the challenging climbs in the area. The Grand Teton and Mount Moran. The Absaroka Range. Parts of the Wind River Range. I even made a trip out one winter to climb the South Fork.

My trip at the end of this summer will be my biggest test yet.

"I'm on a leave of absence," I tell Nick, shifting my eyes to watch his reaction. "I'm taking extra time at the end of the summer to do Gannett Peak."

I've been on nine-month contracts with my company every year since they hired me out of college. The pay is decent enough for an entry-level position, and I keep my expenses low except for unavoidably high rent and student loans, plus my climbing trips and gear.

But the summer is the best time to climb. I work here at B&B for some income and because it puts me within easy access to multiple challenging and just-for-fun climbs. Plus, the people, of course.

Nick lets out a low whistle. "For real? I'm not even gonna lie, man, that's impressive. What's the hike to get to the climb, like fifteen miles or something?"

I grin, my eyes drifting to the peaks in the distance again. "Twenty. And in late August, it's mostly ice." Excitement bubbles up from my stomach to my chest. "I've been planning the trip since college. And this is the year I'm making it happen."

I'll sign another contract with my company this fall, probably a twelve-month one this time around. The real world, as Nick called it, will be my permanent residence soon enough. This will be my last summer at B&B, too.

In six months when I turn twenty-five, I'll get access to a trust fund with the modest assets left by my mom after all her medical bills and funeral expenses. It's not much but will be enough for a down payment to buy my own house—my own home. The real estate market is expensive in Boulder, and it could take me years to save up enough money for the down payment on my own. I'm eager to feel settled.

But that's all a problem for later. The next two months, other than my responsibilities here at B&B, my sole focus is on preparing for Gannett. My days off will consist of quick trips to some of the easier climbs in the area so I can stay sharp.

A laugh rings out from the other end of the corral where some of the wranglers are pulling the saddles and other tack out of storage.

My gaze snags on Taylor. Her honey-brown hair is braided into pigtails that hang over her shoulders. She's smiling and laughing at something one of the other women said. My eyes follow her curves down to her jean-clad legs, and I swallow as I try to dismiss how much I like the way she looks.

Nick clears his throat, and I realize I've been staring a little too long.

"What do you think of the new staff this summer?" he asks, his voice casual.

I shrug, turning back to my work. "They seem nice but that's no surprise. George and Pamela always hire the friendliest people."

"Yeah, nice. Pretty, too."

I look at him from where I'm crouched on the ground next to the fence. "Don't you have a girlfriend back home?"

"I do. But *you* don't." He smirks. "At least not that I'm aware of."

He's right. I'm definitely single, but also not looking. It's obvious he's got some little matchmaking scheme in mind, and I'm not interested.

I grunt in response and focus back on prying the broken rail off the post.

His laugh is short and deep. "I'll take that as a maybe."

I wish he'd take it as a "no." I'm committed to casual dating—preferably away from the close quarters of B&B Ranch—and a serious relationship is not on my radar.

I want that someday—a steady girlfriend that turns into a proposal, a wedding, and a house full of kids. But not for years yet. I have many more mountains to climb—literally—before I can think about settling down. My hobbies are too dangerous, and it wouldn't be fair to have a family only to make them worry about me all the time.

Maybe it's obvious that Taylor's caught my eye. But it's also obvious that she's the kind of woman you marry, not the kind you fool around with to pass the summer. I'm better off keeping my distance.

AFTER DINNER, THE STAFF all gather in the "saloon," which is a lounge-type space next to the dining room with a bar area, seating, and games like pool and foosball. Taxidermied animals hang on the walls—a deer head with antlers, a bison head, even an otter perched on a ledge. Near the fireplace, a bear skin is mounted on the lacquered wood-plank wall above a pile of logs and kindling.

With no television or internet available on the ranch, this room is the primary entertainment spot for staff and guests alike. It's a great place for us to gather to get to know each other better. Once the guests arrive, it's part of our responsibilities to be in the saloon after dinner at least two nights a week to encourage games among our visitors, answer questions, and even spin a yarn or two.

Tonight, I join a game of hearts ongoing at one of the round wooden tables. Nick is at the pool table with Jake, one of the new activity guides I haven't gotten to know yet. A group of wranglers sit in the black leather chairs near the fireplace talking excitedly.

George and Pamela watch the activity from the corner near the bar, perched on stools with their eyes shining. They love this place, and especially the way it brings people together every summer: college-aged kids from all over the country to staff the positions, and couples and families from all over the world who stay a week or two at a time as guests wanting a real Western experience.

I know before too long, they'll sneak out to go upstairs to their apartment and leave us to our own devices.

Another round of cards and I'll call it a night, myself. I'm not planning to stay up too late. The horses arrive tomorrow, making for a tiring and busy day.

"Room for one more?" a voice bubbles from over my shoulder.

I turn my head to find Taylor hovering, watching the cards on the table with interest.

Before I can answer her, Danny, one of the activity guides who is new this summer, speaks up. "Sure thing. Pull up a chair, and we'll switch to five-player."

He gathers the cards on the table into a pile and sifts through them to find and remove the two of diamonds and two of spades. Then he shuffles the remaining cards.

Meanwhile, Taylor pulls one of the heavy wooden chairs from another table into the gap between me and Danny, to my left. It's a tight fit, though, and when she sits, her shoulder brushes mine. I scoot my chair more to the right, a flare of annoyance shooting through my chest.

I don't want to be so attracted to her, but I am, and it's aggravating.

"We're playing hearts," I tell Taylor. "Do you know how to play?"

She cocks her head to the side. "Tell me."

"Each player gets ten cards. The goal is to finish the game with the lowest score possible, so you want to avoid the point cards: hearts and the queen of spades. We'll start by passing two cards to the player to the left. You can pick any two from your dealt hand. Then we'll play tricks until all the cards have been played. Watch."

Danny deals the cards. I have two clubs, and three or four of each other suit.

"Choose two cards from your deck to pass. You want to try to get rid of the high cards."

I pass the two club cards to Taylor and accept two cards from Makayla to my right. Keeping my face as passive as possible, I'm mentally doing a victory dance. Makayla didn't pass me any clubs, and because I got rid of the two I started with, this first trick is going to give me a major advantage.

Anna has the two of clubs, so she sets it in the middle of the table.

"If you have a club, you have to play it. The person who plays the highest card in the leading suit each trick wins that trick, but that's not necessarily a good thing because if there are point cards in the mix, you'll end up with them and run up your score. But nobody can play point cards in the first trick. The winner of the trick also has to start the next trick."

Makayla plays the five of clubs, then I put down the king of spades. If there's a spade trick later in the hand, now I won't be at risk of winning it and getting the queen of spades, which is worth thirteen points.

Danny hisses. “No clubs?”

I smirk at him.

Taylor considers her cards. She starts to pick one out of her hand, then stops and fingers another.

She finally plucks a card from her hand and sets it on the table. Ace of clubs.

I cringe. She really is a beginner.

“You probably don’t want to play that high of a club card on the first trick,” Makayla explains to her gently.

Taylor blinks. “But if no one can play point cards yet, I won’t get any points for winning, right?”

“Well, yeah, technically, but now you’ll have to lead the next trick.”

“And that’s bad?”

This time Anna answers her. “It can be because you don’t know what cards everyone else has.”

“Oh, okay. Sorry.”

We finish out the trick, and Taylor takes the cards and piles them in front of her on the table. She pulls a card from her hand and sets it on the table to start the next trick.

Ace of spades.

I audibly groan, and Taylor turns toward me. “What? Was that wrong?”

I clear my throat. “It’s an interesting strategy, that’s for sure.”

Danny plays the queen of spades, and I point at the card.

“Because of that,” I say. “Now, you’re going to win the trick and rack up thirteen points from that little lady right there.”

Taylor bites her bottom lip and stares at the cards in the center of the table. “Oh.”

We keep playing tricks as the number of cards in our hands dwindles. Unfortunately, Taylor doesn't seem to be getting the hang of the game. She's won more tricks than not.

We're on the final trick before I realize what's happening. I pick up the cards I've won and shuffle through them—no hearts. I think back through the game and try to remember who did win tricks with hearts in them. Did . . . anybody?

It can't be.

When it's my turn, I throw down my last card: a seven of diamonds. Everyone's out of hearts by now, so it's a garbage trick that Makayla ends up winning.

As everyone else at the table picks up their piles of cards to start adding up their points, I watch Taylor. Is she . . . smirking?

We didn't explain to her that if a player gets all the point cards in a hand, it's called "shooting the moon" and results in the player with all the point cards getting zero points and everyone else getting twenty-six points each. It's one of the riskiest strategies in the game because if you miss even a couple of hearts, you end up with a high point total for the hand.

Usually, it's easy to spot a player shooting the moon because they might lead a high card on the second trick. That's a huge tell that they're trying to shoot the moon, and the other players can fight back to sabotage them.

Taylor led the second trick with the ace of spades. We all assumed it was a mistake, but maybe—

"Guys," I say quietly, waiting until Danny, Anna, and Makayla look at me. "Does *anyone* have hearts?"

Their expressions are pure confusion as they look through their cards and come up blank. We all turn to Taylor.

She leans back in her chair, the cutest smug look on her face. "Call me John F. Kennedy, because I just shot the moon."

The table explodes with shouts of laughter and surprise.

My mouth drops open. Did she . . . was she . . . she *hustled* us? At hearts?

Taylor looks so pleased with herself, and I get the wildest impulse to kiss that self-satisfied smirk off her lips.

I picture myself leaning in, taking her bottom lip between mine, and kissing her until she's as shocked and confused and . . . and . . . *affected* as I feel right now.

Instead, I shake my head and clear my throat. I force a casual smile onto my face.

"Well played, Taylor." I turn to Danny. "Ready to deal the next hand?"

Everyone passes Danny their cards; he shuffles the deck and starts dealing.

I take each card he passes to me and fan them out in my hand. I don't see them, though. I'm watching Taylor out of the corner of my eye, my head spinning.

I might be in trouble here.

Chapter Five

Taylor

The alarm on my phone wakes me at seven, and I sit up in bed *still* glowing after my total domination in hearts last night. After I shot the moon in the first hand, we finished out that game, and then played a second and third, staying up later than I think any of us intended.

That was fun.

Hearts is an absolute institution in the retirement community where my grandmother has lived for the past ten years. Every Friday night, Grammy and I walk to the clubhouse and sit around a table with a revolving set of challengers in a tournament-style showdown. I don't always play, but when I do, it's typical for Grammy and me to face off in the championship game.

You might say she's taught me everything I know. About cards, for sure, but about a lot of other things, too.

Including horses.

Of course, I learned from my parents as I helped them manage the horse farm growing up, but before the farm was theirs, it was Grammy's. She and my grandpa started Steed Farm and ran it for decades until Grandpa passed away when I was eleven.

Grammy stayed on for a while after that, but the memories—mostly good, but all bittersweet as she grieved the love of her life—overwhelmed her, she said, and she needed a fresh start.

I wish I could call her this morning. I know she'd share my excitement about meeting twenty new horses today and starting the process of getting to know each one.

But no cell service on the ranch means phone calls are limited to the evening hours when staff can use the office phone for personal calls or to the days when I can make it back toward town.

It's the first thing I'll do on my next day off.

I heard Becca up and about earlier, and she's already gone by the time I haul myself out of bed. This will be my last day sleeping in for a while, so I make the most of it. Starting tomorrow, the other wranglers and I will be seeing to the horses' breakfast before our own, plus wellness checks and paddock maintenance every morning.

I shower and dress quickly for breakfast. When I'm ready to go, I peek out the front door, but no bison friends are grazing there today.

Eyes closed, I stifle a sleepy yawn as I step off the front porch of my cabin. When I open my eyes again, there's Jackson, halfway up the path between his cabin and mine, looking not unlike a proverbial deer in the headlights. Surprised and maybe . . . annoyed?

Is he upset about my little hustle last night? It was all in fun; I didn't mean any harm.

Still, despite his less-than-enthusiastic expression, my heart gallops in my chest. He's hatless, his wavy brown hair curling against his forehead.

Jeans and dark leather cowboy boots. He's got his hoodie on again, though in my opinion it's much too cold for a hoodie to do anything useful. I'm wearing my coat and contemplating pulling the gloves out of my pocket to put on, too.

"Good morning!" I chirp, offering him a smile.

"Mornin'," he replies.

As he reaches me, I fall into step beside him. "Are you excited that the horses are getting here today?"

He shrugs. "I guess. I'll help where I can, but I'm not much of a horseman."

I stop walking as he continues down the path, and my hand flies to my chest. "'Not much of a horseman'? You work at a guest ranch! For several summers now, I hear. How can you not be 'much of a horseman'?"

He stops and without turning around, shrugs again. "Just not."

Jackson starts walking again, but I hang back, confused. I don't understand his clipped responses and surly demeanor.

Two days ago, when Jackson and I first met in orientation, *he* approached *me*. He was sweet and friendly. Then I hear from Becca and the other returners that he's such a nice guy and welcoming and considers himself an ambassador for the ranch.

Yesterday morning, he stood on my front porch and told me about bison. Again, he was friendly and helpful.

Is he having a bad morning? Or is this about . . . me? About my con playing cards last night.

"Are you mad about hearts last night?" I call down the path. I haven't moved yet, and he's several yards in front of me now. "I'm sorry. We weren't playing for money or anything, so I didn't think it was a big deal. I didn't mean to upset anyone."

He turns, and his expression has shifted—less irritated now and more contrite, though still a little pained.

"No. I'm sorry, Taylor. I'm not mad about hearts or anything else. I'm . . . not myself this morning. But it's not you."

I tilt my head and study him, distracted by the way the morning sunlight catches in his eyes, illuminating flecks of copper, like pieces of shiny pennies.

"Okay, thanks," I finally say, and he waits for me to catch up. We continue walking toward the lodge together.

Jackson clears his throat. "Actually, last night you were . . . impressive. I didn't see your moon shot coming until it was too late. Where'd you learn to play hearts like that?"

My silly heart soars with his praise. I remind myself to calm down, but there's no denying how pleased I am. I feel the blush all over my face.

"Me and my grammy sort of dominate a hearts syndicate in her retirement community," I admit.

He raises his eyebrows. "What now?"

I laugh and entertain him with stories of the questionable happenings at Hillgarden Senior Living the rest of the way to the lodge for breakfast.

THE STARS IN MY eyes are probably obvious as I watch one horse after another make their way out of the trailers and into our fenced-in pasture here at the ranch.

Gorgeous horses. Quarter horses and paints. Pintos and draft crosses. In a variety of sizes and colors: bays, grays, blacks, piebalds, and more.

Pamela stands at the gate, checking each horse off from the list on the clipboard in her hands. The horses are identified by their markings, their names listed on the paperwork from their home ranch. George removes their halters before he lets them off the trailer and through the gate, so they don't snag on anything and cause injury.

These horses look built for the mountain terrain. They have large hooves and hefty, muscular bodies. They're also, I'm told, trained to work with riders of all skill levels. I'm eager to take each and every one for a test ride.

The other wranglers and I watch closely to monitor the social hierarchy of the herd, trying to identify the alpha and readying ourselves to intervene in case any of the scuffles get too heated.

We're also checking for any signs of injury—limping, heat in their legs—anything that might signal a thrown shoe or sore foot.

Staff hover outside the pasture, patrolling the fence line as the horses run the perimeter. The weak points of the fence were repaired yesterday, but if the staff missed any spots, the horses will find them.

A few yards to my left, two geldings scuffle, feigning nips at each other. One is large and gray and the other a smaller bay. They're playing, but the bay keeps coming back and agitating the larger horse. Before I can intervene, a sorrel mare walks over, her ears flat back and her nostrils tight, staring them down.

The geldings dash away, and I understand that this old girl is the alpha.

We work with the horses the rest of the day, with a short break for lunch in the early afternoon. I quickly have my favorites.

Mesa is a bay mare with a blaze of white across her face. She's sneaky and playful and loves to stretch her neck through the fence to munch on wildflowers outside the pasture.

Pistol is a chestnut mare with stockings. She's a troublemaker and does not like other horses behind her. She gives them a warning tail swish, and if they don't move, she'll kick.

My guess is the same will apply to people, so I make a note on the chalkboard in the pole barn next to Pistol's name.

The other wranglers have added their notes about the various horses as well: gentle, bossy, curious, calm, social. When we think one will be good with kids, we put a star next to their name. We'll adjust and readjust these impressions before the guests arrive. As the horses settle in, we'll have a chance to ride them and learn more about their personalities.

I've felt more in my element today than any other since I arrived in Wyoming. Between the tall mountain landscapes, the cold weather, and the new people, my summer so far has been a lot of novelty.

I love people, and I enjoy new experiences, but working with horses is the same everywhere. The herds are different, as are the personalities of the individual horses, but the work is familiar and comforting. It feels like home, even though I'm two thousand miles from everything I know.

After dinner, I pry my boots off my feet and wash the dust from my skin, then fall into bed.

My cabin's on the other side of the ranch from the corral, but I still swear I can hear the nickers and soft chuffs of the herd as I drift off to sleep.

Chapter Six

Taylor

THE NEXT MORNING IS more of the same. Me and the other wranglers—Becca, Ashley, and Samantha, plus our lead wrangler Leanne—are out tending to the horses as soon as we wake up, before breakfast is available in the dining room.

After they eat, we can finally eat, and we make our way to the lodge.

As I heap scrambled eggs and bacon onto my plate, I notice Jackson sitting with some of the other men, including his roommate, Nick. I want to say hi and let Jackson's smile power me through the rest of my day, but I hold back. He hasn't said a word to me since we arrived at the lodge together for breakfast yesterday.

Not that I think he's intentionally avoiding me, of course. We were all busy yesterday getting the horses settled, after all. And why should he go out of his way to talk to me? We're not friends. We've had a few nice moments, but anything more than that is in my head. Wishful thinking on account of my stupid crush on him.

I find Becca and join her table, deliberately sitting with my back to Jackson so I'm not tempted to sneak glances.

After breakfast, each of the wranglers pick a horse, and we take them for a trail ride up the mountain.

Leanne tells us about the four horse trails that are close to the ranch and perfect for guest rides. I'm the only new wrangler—the other three are returners, though Becca and Samantha were cabin wranglers last summer, so this is their first time working solely with the horses. Becca told me that they helped the wranglers whenever they could last summer, so they'd be more prepared to be full wranglers this summer.

The trail we take today follows Libby Creek up the mountain past downed trees and fields of wildflowers. After a ways, we leave the creek and continue across a green meadow. Ahead of us, the horizon line bends as if we're in the dip of a *V*, the earth angling up on either side of us. Beyond that are layer upon layer of mountains. The ones closest to us are green and tree covered. Behind the taller peaks covered in snow, the cloudless blue sky reflects off them in a way that makes me wish I'd worn my sunglasses.

For someone who's lived her whole life on the flat, low-lying land of Florida, the landscape here is stunning and exotic.

"There was a huge forest fire up here about ten years ago," Leanne calls back over her shoulder as our horses lumber behind hers. "That's why you see so many downed and blackened trees."

"Ten years?" I muse. "Wouldn't the dead trees have decomposed by now?"

"Good question, but no. The high-altitude means colder temperatures, dry conditions, and fewer microorganisms like fungi to break down the wood. It could take these trees decades to fully decompose."

Start to finish, the trail ride takes us three hours. The horses we chose are impressively well behaved and walk together well. When we return to the pole barn, we update the chalkboard with our observations about the horses we rode and their demeanors.

My horse, Mesa, was a gem. I draw a star by her name to indicate she'll be great with kids.

THE NEXT FEW DAYS pass like this—up early to tend to the horses, trail rides with different horses each morning and afternoon—until we've ridden all the horses and learned all the trails.

Saturday morning at breakfast, we're ready for a day off, and this is the only one we'll have all together all summer. Each employee gets two days off a week, but they rotate so that the ranch is always staffed. Once orientation is over, guests will arrive on Sunday afternoons and leave on Saturday mornings. In between, the cabins are turned over, and the ranch is prepared for the next round of guests.

The horses need tending every day, of course, though with four wranglers and Leanne, when one or even two wranglers have a day off, the others can manage. Pamela explained that most often, the wranglers are off Wednesdays or weekends because there are fewer trail rides to lead on those days. Wednesdays because that's the day most guests go on the tour of Yellowstone National Park. Some may stay behind to get more riding in, but we don't all need to be here.

George stands and claps his hands loudly. "Everyone, I need a couple of volunteers to take one of the ranch vans down to Cody for supplies and a refueling this morning."

Jackson raises his hand, and then, without my arm communicating with my brain, my hand is raised, too.

George points to each of us. "Jackson, Taylor. Perfect. That works well to pair up one of our long-time returners with one of our newest staff members."

Jackson turns in his seat to look at me, and my face burns. *Stupid crush.* Why did I volunteer? More time with Jackson, especially one-on-one, is not going to help me get over this crush, and I need to. It's embarrassing.

"When you finish eating, go find Pamela in the office, and she'll give you the keys and a ranch credit card," George says.

It's an hour drive down to Cody and an hour drive back. I volunteered to spend two hours stuck in a van with Jackson.

What was I thinking?

I MEET JACKSON BY the vans, and we load up. If he's annoyed I volunteered to come with him, he doesn't show it. The Jackson I'm getting today is the friendly ranch ambassador.

He starts driving us down the mountain, and once again, I'm mesmerized by the landscape. For much of the drive, the road runs next to the Shoshone River on the passenger side of the van. I watch the water splash against rocks as it speeds along, hoping I'll see a bear or a deer or some other type of wildlife.

Jackson's quiet, letting me enjoy the view, and he turns the radio to a local oldies rock station.

After we've been driving for thirty minutes, my phone starts going crazy from inside my coat, and Jackson chuckles.

"Yep. This is about the spot where we're in range for cell service again."

I pluck my phone gleefully from my pocket and survey the notifications. I've never thought of myself as someone addicted to their phone—I use mine way less than most of my friends back home—but after days of no connectivity, the dopamine hit is satisfying.

Most of the notifications are from social media sites, but I have a few texts, too. Before I left, Grammy told me that she would keep texting me like normal, even though she knows I won't see the messages right away.

There's one from my mom, too: "Not urgent, but call me when you get the chance."

Even though she says it's not urgent, my hands start sweating. *Is Grammy okay?* I scroll through Grammy's texts, but they only show when I received them, not when they were sent.

"Do you mind if I call my mom?" I ask.

Jackson turns down the radio. "Not at all."

I wait as the line rings, and my mom finally picks up. "Taylor honey! Hi! How's Wyoming?"

"It's great. I saw your text that I should call?" I brace myself for whatever she's going to say.

"Oh, yeah, I wanted to see how things are going!"

My shoulders sag, and I wipe a hand over my face. "Mom! I thought something was wrong!"

"I said it wasn't urgent," she retorts, lengthening the vowels in "said." I picture the wrinkle I'm sure is between her eyebrows.

"Grammy's okay?" I ask to confirm.

"Grammy's great. She was here for dinner last night."

I exhale. "Okay."

"But tell me what you've been up to! Where are you now?"

I run through the high points of my week, giving her more details than the average person would likely want about each of the horses, but I know Mom will appreciate them.

"And right now, I'm driving to town in one of the ranch vans to run errands for the owners."

I hear a small gasp. "On those mountain roads? Taylor, you should not be talking on the phone. You need to focus!"

I chuckle. "No, Mom, I'm in the passenger seat. My coworker is driving." I switch the phone to speaker and hold it up. "Say 'hi,' Jackson."

Jackson looks at the phone and the corners of his mouth quirk up. "Hi, Mrs. . . ."

"Steed," I stage whisper.

He grins. "Hi, Mrs. Steed."

"Hello, young man!"

"Jackson," I remind her.

"Jackson," she repeats. "I hope you're driving safely. You have precious cargo on board, you know."

I roll my eyes. "Mom!"

Jackson smiles again. "Yes, ma'am, Mrs. Steed. I've been driving mountain roads for years."

He winks at me, and I almost drop the phone. My stomach dips, and I barely manage to stifle a mindless giggle.

"Gotta go, Mom. Tell Dad I said hello. I'll call Grammy before we go back to the ranch."

"All right, honey. Love you!"

I end the call and busy myself reading through Grammy's text messages. I don't look at Jackson.

After a beat, he laughs. "Wait, so your last name is Steed, and you own a horse farm? That's a little too perfect."

My cheeks warm, and I smile. I *love* this story. "Actually, my last name is Steed-Gallagher. The Gallagher is from my dad, and the Steed is from my mom. It was her parents who started the farm."

"My point still stands. The *Steeds* have a horse farm."

I laugh, my lips pressed together so it vibrates through my throat. "Their last name is exactly why they chose to start a horse farm over pretty much any other kind of business. They didn't know anything about horses when they started it."

Jackson glances at me, his eyebrows raised. "You're kidding."

I shake my head. "I'm not. When they first got married, they moved around a lot. Nomadic, my grandmother called it. They wanted to see everything, do everything. They lived that way for ten years, never staying in the same place too long. Then, one day they decided they'd done enough and wanted to settle down. Problem was, they didn't know what to do. Grammy joked about starting a horse farm, and it went from there."

"That's amazing."

"Yeah, they researched the industry and decided to settle in Ocala and breed racehorses. Steed Farm was born only a year before my mother."

"Your grandparents sound awesome."

"Yeah. My grandpa passed away a while ago, though."

Jackson doesn't say anything. I turn my head, thinking maybe he didn't hear me. He's staring straight ahead out the windshield, so it's hard to see his face, but his jaw is tight. Like maybe I said something that hit a nerve.

"Jackson? You okay?"

He inhales, a quick sniff. "Fine," he answers. "I'm sorry about your grandpa."

"Thanks. It's been hard on Grammy. She's doing better now than when he first passed, but—"

"It never really gets better," Jackson finishes.

He sounds like someone with his own experience with grief, and I wonder who he's lost in his life.

"Yeah, not really," I say softly.

He sniffs again and clears his throat. "Anyway, did you get to spend much time in Cody before you came up to the ranch?"

I saw the airport and my hotel near the airport. My flight got in late, and I was exhausted. "Not really, no."

"It's small, but it has some neat shops and a surprising number of art galleries and museums. I don't know what you have planned for your day off today . . . I mean, if you want to get back to the ranch as soon as possible, or . . ."

I turn my head to look at Jackson. He keeps his eyes on the road, but the tips of his ears are red. It seems like he's . . . inviting me to spend the day with him. But that can't be right. Unless his role as unofficial ranch ambassador extends to showing people around Cody, too.

"I'm not in a rush," I tell him.

He whooshes out a breath. "Okay, well then maybe we could spend some time in Cody today? We can check out some of the galleries, get some lunch."

A warm glow extends out from my chest. "Yeah, that sounds nice."

Chapter Seven

Jackson

Somehow my resolve to keep my distance from Taylor has turned into suggesting we spend the day together, just the two of us.

And I don't think I regret it.

Nothing on Pamela's list of supplies needs refrigeration, so we go to the store first and get the ranch business taken care of. Then, I park in one of the public lots downtown so we can explore the area on foot.

I've been to Cody plenty of times, of course. Though I'm more likely to spend my days off farther up the mountain than in town, I've seen most of Cody, including all the Buffalo Bill Center of the West museums and the Old Trail Town collection of historic buildings.

It's different, though, seeing it through Taylor's eyes. Many of the storefronts are set up like an old Western main street, with a mixture of the practical and the entertaining. A boot shop, a pharmacy, but also a bookstore and at least six art galleries.

Taylor leads us into the first art gallery we pass. We're greeted by a large oil painting of the local scenery, brush strokes evident in the textured sky. The next one, a winter scene of hay bales stacked by a fence and covered in snow. Taylor lingers here for several moments, her eyes tracking over the canvas in a pattern, as if she doesn't want to miss a single inch.

"Have you ever been here in the winter?" she asks.

I glance at the white sky and ground in the painting. "Yeah, a couple of years ago."

"Is it like this?" She gestures to the canvas. "Covered in snow?"

I'm quiet as I remember. "Not here in town. There can be snow, but it's not constant. As you go up the mountains more, closer to the ranch and Yellowstone, yeah. The river up that way turns to ice. Not totally, but chunks of it. To the south, too. I climbed the South Fork the winter before last, and the Shoshone was frozen solid." I smile. "That was lucky for me, because otherwise I'd have had to wade through the freezing water to get to the base."

I'm focusing on the white sky of the painting as I talk but slowly realize that Taylor is staring at me. I shift my gaze and take in her widened eyes.

"What do you mean *climbed the South Fork*? What is it?"

I bite my bottom lip as I consider how to describe it. "The South Fork is a section of the Shoshone River. It has these amazing volcanic cliffs with jagged peaks and tall, vertical walls. Lots of waterfalls. In the winter, the waterfalls freeze solid, like giant icicles hanging from the rock."

"So, you climb the walls?"

I huff a laugh. "We climb the frozen waterfalls."

She blinks once, then again, then takes a step back. "You *what*?"

"Yep." I grin. I'm used to this kind of shocked reaction when I talk about my hobby. Still, I like the impressed glint in Taylor's eyes a little too much.

I pull out my phone and scroll through my photos until I find one my buddy took of me halfway up Hells Angel, one of the more prominent ice climbs in the South Fork. I hold the screen toward Taylor, and she gapes.

"Is that you?"

"That's me."

"That's amazing! How beautiful!" She blushes and splutters, "I mean, the waterfall is beautiful. Not, like *you* are beautiful. I mean, I can't even tell it's you. It looks like a red blob with legs, you know? So, yeah . . . the ice . . . looks beautiful."

She looks at the ground, holding her hands over her cheeks.

I hesitate. On the one hand, knowing Taylor might be attracted to me like I am to her leaves me breathless. On the other hand, it kind of makes my problem worse. It's one thing to tuck away my interest for a woman who sees me as a coworker or a friend. It's another thing entirely to fight a mutual attraction.

Either way, though, I don't want her to feel embarrassed now. I stoop so we're face-to-face and smile. "I know what you meant, and you're right. The waterfall is gorgeous."

She returns my smile, and we stand there smiling at each other a little bit too long.

WE MAKE OUR WAY down the street and pop into a few more galleries. Watching Taylor look at the artwork is the highlight of my day. I can appreciate a pretty painting or cool sculpture, but I don't know anything about how it was created or the techniques used or anything like that. Taylor does. She doesn't just look at the art; she studies it.

And I make a study of her while she does it. Not intentionally. We're walking together, and then we stop to look at a piece of art. I'm done with it in a few seconds, but she lingers, and I find my eyes drifting to her face instead of the artwork in front of us. The way her eyes track over the piece. The way she bites her top lip as she considers it. The way she gets so lost in the art that I can stare at her, and she doesn't even notice.

Seeing her intense focus, her satisfaction, gives me this little jolt of joy. I don't know why; I don't even know her. I think it's that the pleasure she gets from studying the artwork is so uncomplicated, and I'm envious. Nothing about my emotions has felt uncomplicated since my mother died six years ago.

We step back onto the sidewalk after exploring another gallery, and Taylor stops, grabbing my arm.

"Look!" She points across the street. "A soda saloon!"

I follow her finger to a café housed in a brick building with a large retro blade sign advertising old-fashioned soda and ice cream. I've been there a handful of times over the years and know they also serve sandwiches and salads.

"You want to stop in for lunch and check it out?"

Her face lights up, and again I'm impressed with how easily she's delighted.

We cross the street at the next intersection and enter the restaurant that's set up as a cross between a retro soda shop and an old Western saloon.

Taylor sits on a stool at the bar, and I slide onto the stool next to her. We order lunch and a flight of sodas—six small glasses where we choose which of the saloon's thirty unique flavors to order—to share. She picks three flavors and I pick three flavors, but we both try all six. My favorite is the cinnamon soda, which tastes a little spicy. Taylor likes the sour green river flavor, which is like a sour lime.

We take our time, talking and getting to know each other better. She tells me more about her artwork, and I reminisce about the flight time I had to log to get my pilot's license.

Taylor loves to paint. She loves watercolors and oils and especially loves to sit in bright sunlight as she creates. Her favorite subject, not surprisingly, is horses. She shows me pictures on her phone of some of her most recent paintings.

"This is my horse Serena." She leans the screen toward me, swiveling on her stool until her knees bump the side of my leg. She leaves them there, not moving away, so I don't either. I peer at the photo on her phone of a light brown horse with a dark mane and tail.

"What kind of horse is that?" I ask. Swallowing thickly, I try to focus on the conversation and not on the warmth of where the fabric of her jeans scrapes against mine.

"She's a Paso Fino." I lift my eyebrows in question, and she continues. "Paso Fino are Spanish horses. They're known for their smooth gaits. We have a lot of them in Florida, especially in Ocala. Paso Finos are the specialty of my family's farm."

I shrug, but I find that I'm interested in hearing more about Taylor's horses. "I don't actually know much about horses," I admit.

She pins me with a curious look, leaning forward. "You mentioned that you're not much into horses. I wondered if there's a story there."

Of course there's a story there, but as much as I'm drawn to Taylor, I still don't know her well. I'm not ready to spill my guts. "Maybe one for another time."

She shifts back on her stool, blushing. Her knees shift away with her, and my leg feels cold in the spot where we were touching. "Of course. I didn't mean to be pushy. Sorry."

"No, no. You weren't. It's just . . ." I pull out my phone and look at the time. "We've got more Cody to see."

I pay for lunch, despite Taylor's protests, and we're back to walking. We're near a Western outfitter, and I expect we'll walk on past to another art gallery on the other side, but Taylor tugs my arm.

"Let's go in," she urges.

I'm content to follow where she leads, so I gesture for her to go ahead, and I trail behind her into the store.

"I need a new hat," she explains as she cranes her neck to find the hat section of the store.

"What's wrong with the hat you brought?" I remember seeing her in a cute hat with decorative holes along the top and some sort of beading around the base.

"It's straw," she says, like that explains everything.

I have a Stetson I bought when I first started working at B&B. George and Pamela like guests to have the full Western experience, so they ask all of us to wear jeans with hats and boots, even a big belt buckle and bolo tie if we're so inclined, which I am not.

"Okay?"

"I need a felt hat," she explains. "We don't use felt hats at home because they're too heavy in the heat and humidity. I'd be drowning in my own sweat after an hour. But no one wears straw hats here. I want to fit in."

I figure she'll roll her eyes at me if I admit I hadn't noticed a difference, so I stay quiet.

Taylor picks a dark brown hat with turquoise detailing, pays for it, and puts it on right away.

"How do I look?" she asks.

Amazing, of course. I haven't yet seen her when she doesn't look amazing.

"It's cute," I tell her. "Very Wyoming."

WE STOP AT A gas station on our way back to the ranch. There's a place halfway between B&B and Cody that gives the ranch a discount if we buy a certain amount of gas per month, so it's where George always wants us to fill up the vans.

Taylor gets out to stretch her legs while I go inside to register the ranch's discount. I come back in time to see a seedy thirty-something man in jeans and a tank top approach Taylor.

"You like ridin' horses?" he asks, but he says it like "hurses." It's an accent I don't recognize, but it's not local.

Taylor blinks up at him.

I'm by her side in a flash. "Is there a problem?" I ask the guy.

He looks me up and down. I may not be the tallest guy, but I'm muscular. I have to be to pull myself up mountains.

Finally, he responds. "Nah, we're good." He walks back to his clunker of a truck and drives away.

Taylor regards me with wide eyes. "What was that about? That guy was just asking me about horses."

I groan. "Taylor, there's no way you're *that* naive."

Her cheeks blush pink. "Well, let's pretend I am for a second."

I take off my ball cap and run my hand through my hair with another groan I feel deep in my chest. "That guy was hitting on you. And not like 'Oh, there's a pretty girl, let me shoot my shot' kind of hitting on you. He didn't really mean horses." I raise my eyebrows to punctuate my meaning.

Taylor's whole face turns scarlet. "Oh," she says in a tiny voice.

She retreats back to her seat in the van while I pump the gas. As I do, I wonder, *how old is Taylor?* She must be at least nineteen. B&B generally hires staffers who have completed at least one year of college.

In some ways, she seems older than that, though. She's competent enough of a horsewoman to be hired as a wrangler her first summer here. The paintings she showed me on her phone reflected a certain depth of emotion I wouldn't expect from a nineteen-year-old.

In other ways, like her innocence in the face of that creepy guy's attention, she seems young. Although all the B&B staffers have been seeming younger and younger to me lately. It's one reason why I know this has to be my last summer at the ranch. I'm not some old fogey or anything—I'm still in my early twenties myself—but to me there's a gaping chasm between a twenty-four-year-old like me and a nineteen-year-old, even if it is only five years.

Back in the van, I pull out onto the road.

We're quiet for a couple of miles, and then Taylor asks, "You think I'm pretty?"

She's not being coy—I'm not sure she knows how to be—and her voice is more curious than anything else.

I clear my throat. "There's no *thinking* about it; it's a fact. You're pretty." It's an understatement really. Taylor is more than pretty.

I keep my gaze trained to the road in front of me, but out of the corner of my eye I see her cheeks turn pink.

"How old are you?" I ask her.

She tips back in her seat at the abruptness of my question, but answers anyway. "Twenty-two. I just graduated from college."

The breath I exhale is in relief, but once again, knowing doesn't make my problem any easier. I'm running out of excuses for why Taylor might not be right for me.

Chapter Eight

Taylor

THE FOLLOWING WEEK IS the last before guests start arriving. To give me and the other wranglers practice leading trail rides, we invite our coworkers to join us. We take groups out in the morning and afternoon, learning the trails and how to deal with problems that might come up on the ride.

With my new felt hat on my head, my morning trail ride on Pistol goes smoothly. Four of the cabin wranglers join me, excited and eager to try riding. A couple of them have ridden before, and one wants to apply to be a wrangler next summer.

I take them on the longer Kitty Creek trail. We cross the road by the ranch entrance and ride along a trail that has our horses splash through a creek in one spot and walk over a wooden bridge in another. The morning is cool—I'm still wearing my flannel-lined jacket—though the sky is clear, and the sun's steady rays are starting to warm us all up.

At lunch back on the ranch, Jackson sits next to me.

We've been enjoying a sort of tentative friendship since our day in Cody together. I say *tentative* because the feelings I'm having toward him are more than friendly. The more I learn about him, the more my crush deepens.

There were a couple of moments on Saturday when I thought maybe he might be interested in me, too. It could also be wishful thinking, convincing my brain of something that's not there, and I'll end up embarrassing myself later because of it.

Yes, unfortunately I am speaking from experience.

I'd like to say I learned my lesson, but I'm nothing if not tenacious. Usually, I know what I want, and I'm not afraid to go for it, even when it leads to abject mortification.

I *have* learned to wait things out a bit more, though. Make sure someone's on the same page before I speak my feelings. Look for signs. Let them make the first move.

So, I'm sticking with friendship with Jackson.

"I didn't see you on the trail rides this morning," I comment as he bites into his sandwich.

He bobs his head, chews, and swallows. "You're very observant."

"Are you coming on one of the afternoon rides?"

"Nope. I'm working on a project for George. Getting all the fishing gear organized ahead of Thursday's trial run."

Oh, disappointing. I know Jackson says he's not much of a horseman—which by the way, I'm still trying to figure that one out because he works on a *ranch*—but it would have been fun to share one of my favorite hobbies with my *friend*.

"That's too bad. The trails are really beautiful. Wildflowers are blooming, birds are chirping. We even saw a marmot this morning!"

He chuckles. "Don't worry, it's impossible to avoid nature altogether out here, even if I wanted to. I don't need to go on a trail ride to enjoy the beauty of the area."

I elbow him in the side. "Okay, but you're missing out."

Internally, I sigh. *Someday I'll get the story out of him about why he doesn't like horses.*

TUESDAY, WE LOAD UP into the ranch vans and drive to Cody to go white water rafting on the Shoshone River. This is an activity that B&B partners with a local company to provide for guests, rather than one of the ones led by camp staff. George and Pamela want us all to try it so we can share our experiences with the guests.

The guide tells us that these are mostly Class I rapids, with a few Class II. That means the rapids are tame, gentle enough that even children can safely participate.

Jackson ends up in the same boat as me. He takes one of the front seats, and I sit down next to him before I can talk myself out of it.

"You're not too busy 'organizing the fishing gear' today?" I tease as I perch on the inflated outer ring of the raft. The guide told us this is the place to sit for the best leverage.

"No way. I never miss rafting. This is the only day we get to go all summer. Well, at least that we don't have to pay for." He winks, taking the paddle the guide hands to him.

"Is white water rafting another of your daredevil hobbies?"

It's my turn to be given a paddle, and I grip it on the top T-shaped handle with one hand, as instructed. The other hand goes lower on the paddle to guide it like a fulcrum. I paid close attention as the guide was giving us instructions. I've never gone white water rafting before, and I'm half thrilled, half anxious about the experience.

Jackson grins. "Nah. It would be fun to navigate some Class V rapids, though. Maybe when I get tired of flying airplanes."

I'm about to ask him more about flying when the rafting guide gives us one last reminder about how to hold our paddles, and we shove off.

Even though we haven't gotten to any waves yet, some of the river water splashes over the edge of the raft onto my feet. I yelp. It's *cold*.

The guides did warn us. They gave us all the option of wearing neoprene booties and wetsuits because they said the river water is only about forty-two degrees right now. Knowing how thin my Florida blood is against the cold, I put on the booties and wetsuit.

But even though my feet are covered with foam high-top socks, I can still feel the stinging chill of the water.

Water splashes onto Jackson's covered feet, too, but he takes it in stride. "You know the front of the boat is more susceptible to splashes, right?" he asks.

That is new information. "No!"

"Yep. You shouldn't have sat here if you didn't want to get wet."

His whole face is shining. Clearly, he sat in front on purpose. So did I, but I'm not about to admit why out loud.

The guide shouts, "Forward two!" and we all obediently put our paddles in the water for two strokes.

In between paddling, I take in the scenery. Jagged red rock cliffs rise up on either side of the river. Above them, the sky is the bluest blue, with puffy clouds suspended like splotches of white paint.

I have my phone with me in a waterproof case. In a calm moment, I pull it out and take a few pictures. This would be so much fun to paint.

I'm already imagining how I'll mix the oil paints to get that perfect shade of blue.

"We're coming up on our first set of rapids!" the guide calls. He shouts instructions, and we paddle. More water sloshes over the side as the raft picks up speed, but I hardly notice this time.

I'm too busy laughing.

I've never considered myself any kind of risk-taker. I ride horses, but I've been doing that so long it feels as natural and safe as walking. My hobbies are quiet ones—painting, reading, playing cards with my grandmother.

But I could get used to this. The thrill of the wind blowing through my hair. The spray of water on my face. The exhilaration of the raft whooshing over the water. I'm sold.

"This is amazing!" I shout to Jackson, my cheeks stretched tight from the wide grin I'm wearing.

He doesn't answer, but he watches me with an expression on his face I can't quite place. Joy, for sure. He's having as much fun as I am, even though this is not his first white water rafting trip, and it's much tamer than scaling frozen waterfalls. But the pink in his cheeks and the bashful bent of his smile make me think there's something else there, too.

The raft bobs over another set of rapids, and I look away from Jackson. Mixed in with my excitement is a warm, peaceful sense of wonder, hot enough in my chest to make my whole body flush.

I've never been much of a risk-taker, but I'm starting to think leaning into my crush on Jackson would be a chance worth taking.

AFTER I PEEL OFF the wetsuit and booties, I sit in the sun and call Grammy. I have a few minutes while I wait for everyone to get ready to go, and I want to take advantage of the cell signal here in Cody while I can.

"Taylor!" Grammy exclaims when she answers the call.

"Hi, Grammy." Hearing her voice makes me simultaneously want to laugh and cry. I'm so glad to talk to her, but it makes me realize how much I miss her, even after only a week and a half away from home.

"How's everything in Wyoming? We all missed you at cards the other night."

I grin and tell her about the game of cards I played last week, how I hustled my way into shooting the moon in hearts.

Her laugh tumbles through the phone line, bright as the sunshine reflecting off the river. "That's my girl!"

"I miss you," I tell her, rubbing a hand over my collarbone as if it will ease the ache in my chest.

"I miss you, too, sweets." She perks up and continues in a teasing voice. "But I'm sure you have plenty of *distractions* in the form of handsome cowboys to keep your mind off an old lady like me."

I blush, thinking of Jackson, who isn't a cowboy but is still handsome enough to keep me distracted.

"Ah-ha. So, there *is* someone?" Though she can't see me through the phone, my pause is long enough to arouse her suspicions, and I hear the smile in her voice.

I hesitate a moment longer, looking around to make sure I'm far enough away from the group that my coworkers don't overhear. Lowering my voice, I answer. "Maybe. I don't know, Gram. I didn't come out here to start a romance." More like I came out here to keep my mind off my lack of romance and experience some new and exciting things.

"The best romances find you when you're not looking," she replies cryptically. "But you have to be brave enough to mount up and take the ride."

I want her to elaborate, but Dennis calls for everyone to load up for the ride back to the ranch.

"Grammy, I have to go. I'm going to lose signal, but I'll try to talk to you again soon. I love you."

"I love you, too, sugar cube. Call when you can."

Becca sits next to me on the drive home. The van is quiet; we're all tired from the excitement of the rafting trip and the early mornings for those of us who are wranglers. Plus, the hard work we've put in at the ranch over the last week and a half.

I shake my head. I've barely started this adventure, and it's already one of my favorite things I've ever done. I may have applied for this job in a moment of panic and desperation, but so far, it's been exactly what I needed.

Chapter Nine

Jackson

THAT FIRST SUNDAY WHEN guests arrive, the excitement in the air is palpable. After lunch, Dennis leaves in one of the ranch vans to pick up the guests that have flown into the Cody airport. Other guests will arrive on their own starting at three, in rental cars or personal vehicles, depending on where they're traveling from.

The grounds, cabins, and lodge are sparkling clean, the staff is trained, the horses are acclimated to the trails, and Chip and Lisa have already started working on a feast for dinner. After two weeks of preparation, we're ready.

The ranch is not at capacity this first week, which is common early in the summer. It's been known to snow in June, and some guests would rather wait until warmth is almost guaranteed.

We have thirty guests coming, including eleven kids. While it's typical for families with kids to stay with us, eleven in one week is higher than normal, especially for a week that's not fully booked.

I love when we have lots of kids at the ranch. Every activity feels more joyful. Kids are more exuberant about trying something new, whether it's hitting the target with an arrow for the first time or hooking a trout in the river. They don't hesitate like adults tend to. That enthusiasm is contagious, and everyone else in the group ends up having more fun, too.

The weather is warm today under the cloudless sky, so I walk back to my cabin to drop off my sweatshirt before the first guests start to arrive.

Taylor is sitting with her nose in a book on the front porch of her cabin. As much as I want to talk to her, I don't want to interrupt her reading.

I'd like to figure Taylor out, but I haven't been able to yet. She likes quiet hobbies like painting and reading, but she also had a blast rafting earlier this week and loves riding horses. It's clear there is some level of adrenaline junkie in her, though not to the extent that I have. I feel compelled to get to know her better, like it's out of my control that I keep getting swept into her orbit.

As friends, of course.

I walk past her cabin, and though I'm on the path several yards away, the disturbance is enough to pull her attention away from her book. She smiles a greeting.

"Aren't you off today?" I ask. "What are you still doing here?"

She stands and places her open book gently onto the chair, the pages spread to hold her place. "I am, but the vans are occupied, and I don't have my own transportation, so I'm hanging out."

Taylor stretches her arms above her head and yawns. Her oversized hoodie lifts, and I linger too long on the way her leggings hug every curve.

Snapping my attention back to her face, I grin. "Tired or relaxed?"

She returns the smile. "I slept in this morning, so relaxed. It's so peaceful out here, especially after a busy week."

We're quiet, both enjoying the calm before the storm of guests arriving. Although, even teeming with guests, the ranch always feels serene.

I notice Taylor looking me up and down the way I did to her a moment ago. George and Pamela like all working staff to be in full cowboy attire on Sundays to welcome the guests. I'm wearing boots, a Stetson, and a large metal belt buckle alongside my jeans and red ranch shirt. Of course, my sweatshirt covers the belt and shirt, but Taylor appears to appreciate the hat and boots, judging by the pink tinging her cheeks while I pretend not to notice her staring.

I'm not usually a fan of cowboy garb, but if wearing it gets this kind of reaction from Taylor, I might have to do it more often.

The sound of tires crunching against the gravel road leading into the ranch breaks the silence.

Jutting my thumb toward the lodge, I say, "All right, well I better get back to it." I wink. "*I'm* not off today. I'll see you at dinner?"

She nods. "Have fun."

As I start to turn away, she flashes a smile that's pure sunshine. Gorgeous sunshine. Taylor has this lightness about her, and I've felt dark inside for so many years now that she draws me in. I'm jealous of her ability to be effortlessly happy.

I've been chasing thrills instead. The exhilaration I feel when I reach the top of a peak or I'm piloting a plane through an electrifying takeoff is satisfying, but it doesn't last. Nothing does.

I'm so caught up in my thoughts and in the stretch of Taylor's lips that I trip over my own feet. I catch myself before I can fall, but my face burns.

"Are you okay?" Taylor calls as I make my escape.

I hold my hand above my head in a thumbs-up. "Yep. All good."

Smooth, Jackson. Real smooth. I'm all the way at the lodge when I realize I never made it to my cabin to drop off my sweatshirt. No way I'm going back now, though.

I yank off my sweatshirt and set it in a corner of the library where I'll hopefully remember to grab it later. Then I walk out to the front porch to help welcome our first arrivals: a man and woman with graying hair and excited smiles.

Pamela welcomes them and walks them to their cabin to settle in.

The other handful of us loitering on the porch relax as we wait for the next batch of guests to arrive.

I settle into a bench seat next to Nick, propping my boots up on the short table in front of us.

The view from the front porch of the lodge is of trees and snowcapped mountains. I'm gazing off into the distance and trying to forget my embarrassment in front of Taylor when I feel Nick's eyes on me.

"What?" I say without looking at him.

"Nothing, just I've never seen you like this before."

I slide my eyes toward him without turning my head. "Like what?"

He harrumphs. "I don't know. Smitten."

I whip around to face him fully. "Smitten?"

Shrugging, he grins at me playfully. "Would you prefer I say twitterpated?"

I glare at him. "Not unless you're an old-timey cartoon character. What are you even talking about?"

"I'm talking about I saw you with Taylor a minute ago." He gives me a knowing look.

A sweat breaks out across my forehead right where the brim of my hat sits. I pull the hat off with one hand and swipe at the moisture with the other.

"You saw me talking to our coworker. So what?"

He huffs and swings his arm onto the top of the cushions behind me. "Please. This is the third summer we've worked here together, and I've *never* seen you talk to a coworker like that before."

I set my feet back on the ground and lean forward, away from Nick. "Like what?"

"Like, falling all over yourself." His mouth quirks up in a grin. "Or almost falling anyway."

Shoot, he saw that? I keep trying to play it off, though. "Look, I don't know what you think you saw, but I'm not smitten or whatever other ridiculous words you're using."

"Protest all you want. You're a friendly guy, Jackson. Always wanting to make sure everyone feels included and comfortable. But the focus you have on Taylor specifically? That's new."

"You're delusional."

He hums. "Okay, then. Name some of the other new staff members here this summer."

Easy. "Danny, Jake—"

Nick interrupts me. "Some of the other new *girls*."

My mind goes blank. *Come on, Jackson.* There were the two other girls who played hearts with us that first night when Taylor hustled us. One of them is . . . blonde, maybe? But what are their names? I shake my head. I always learn everyone's names during orientation.

My chest tightens, and I scowl at Nick. "I don't have to prove anything to you."

He smirks. "No, but you did anyway."

I groan and run a hand down my face. Setting my hat back on my head, I turn away from my friend.

"There's something different about you this summer, man. Before Taylor, even. You seem restless."

"I'm always restless," I mutter.

His voice is thoughtful when he replies. "No. You're always *ready*. Eager for the next adventure, raring to go. This isn't that. It's like you're . . . waiting for something. But maybe you don't know what."

His musings hit their mark. Nick put it into words better than I've been able to. Something does feel different this summer. Maybe because I know it's my last one here at B&B. Or maybe because I'm only months away from this capstone climbing trip I've been planning for years.

Nick continues. "I don't know, man. You've been through a lot. Might be nice to let yourself be happy for a change."

I suck in a breath, meeting Nick's eyes. *He thinks I'm not happy?* I mean, I have a job I love, exciting hobbies that keep me busy when I'm not at work, my own apartment. What more could I need?

"I'm happy," I murmur, suddenly unsure as I turn my gaze to the looming mountains.

"Sorry," Nick says. "I'll back off."

We sit in a loaded silence for too many minutes, and I scramble to shift the mood.

"Taylor's cute," I offer, inwardly cringing at how inadequate the word *cute* feels in describing Taylor. "You're not wrong that I'm attracted to her. But I'm not looking for anything serious."

Nick watches an SUV wind up the road toward the lodge. "Maybe she isn't either."

"Maybe." Though that seems unlikely. Taylor's got *wife* written all over her. Believe me, I don't mean that as a bad thing, just a thing that's not right for me at the moment. I'm not looking for a wife.

The SUV parks, and another middle-aged couple climbs out. Pamela is still away from the lodge with the first couple who arrived, so one of the cabin wranglers—Mary? Maria?—welcomes them as they approach the porch.

"Hello, and welcome to Bear and Bison Ranch! I'm Mia."

Right, Mia. That's her name.

First thing on my mental to-do list is to learn the names of my coworkers. Second is to stop getting distracted by Taylor's smile.

Chapter Ten

Taylor

HAVING THE DAY OFF yesterday was what I needed, because on Monday, the other wranglers and I are *busy*. The guests who plan to ride horses—which is practically all of them—get orientations and safety briefings before we match them with their horses for the week and take them on their first trail rides.

This is my first official trail ride, too—leading one with guests, I mean—and I'm nervous. The practice rounds I did for my coworkers last week went off without a hitch. Still, I hope that I've matched the right horses with the right people and everyone will get along.

Leanne and I are partners to lead a big family group that includes four kids. They're here for a family reunion trip—two grandparents and four couples with eight kids between them—but not all of the children in the family are old enough to ride and not all the adults want to.

We pair up the kids with our gentlest horses and get everyone's saddles adjusted before heading out on one of the easier trails so we can get a sense of the group's comfort level. Leanne has me lead, and she takes up the rear.

It's a gorgeous day. The air is cool enough for me to feel comfortable in jeans and long sleeves—unheard of in Florida in June—but not so cold that I need my jacket. I tilt my hat back to feel the sun on my face for a moment.

Pistol whinnies, and I pat her neck. She's sort of become "my" horse for the summer. She can be more challenging than some of the others, so Leanne wanted an experienced rider to manage her. She's been great for me so far.

Emily, one of the younger kids riding with us, points out the red flowers growing around the trail. "What are those flowers called?" she asks.

With all the trail rides we practiced over the last couple of weeks, I've learned a lot about the local flora. "Those are called Indian paintbrushes. Native Americans have stories about how the Great Spirit used these flowers to paint the sunset."

I glance back at Leanne for confirmation, but I doubt she can hear me from the back of the line.

One of the boys in the group, Bryce, asks about the burnt trees. I explain about the wildfire and how lower oxygen levels up here in the mountains keep the trees from decomposing as quickly.

I'm proud of myself for remembering the details Leanne shared with me back on *my* first B&B trail ride, which seems like ages ago even though it's only been a couple of weeks.

I ask them questions, too, about school and what they like to do for fun. The kids and adults alike chatter happily as we sway down the path, enjoying the landscape and the connection with our horses.

A successful first ride. I'm relieved and pleased and proud that I handled it with minimal help from Leanne.

When we get back to the pole barn, the kids are already begging their parents for another ride after lunch.

We make plans for when to meet this afternoon, and then Leanne and I untack the horses. We check their legs for any issues and pick stones out of their shoes before letting them loose in the pasture to graze and drink.

AT LUNCHTIME, THE DINING room is buzzing with conversation and laughter. Meals are much livelier now that the guests are here. They also come with more expectations because George and Pamela want us to sit with the guests and make conversation with them as part of the B&B Ranch experience.

I scan the room, trying for nonchalance, but Becca knows exactly what I'm doing.

"Jackson's off today," she whispers, leaning in as I pick up a plate at the start of the buffet line.

It makes sense because most of the guests are riding today, so we don't need as many guides handling the other ranch activities.

"Did he go somewhere?" I whisper back. I place a roast beef sandwich on my plate and scoop up a handful of chips with the tongs.

"At breakfast, he and Nick were talking about a climb Jackson was going to do today."

"A climb?"

"Rock climbing," Becca clarifies.

She follows me to a table where we sit with two of the older couples who seem to have become fast friends.

I'm dying to know more about Jackson's mountain climbing. Dying to know more about a lot of things when it comes to him. He and I have talked a lot, but I've started to notice that he directs the conversations back to me whenever he can.

I've talked his ear off about Steed Farm, my parents, Grammy, and all things Florida. Meanwhile, he's told me some things about his hobbies, but little else about his job or family or life back in Colorado. Horses are a sensitive subject, I've learned.

"Taylor." Becca nudges me, and I focus my attention on the guests across from me.

"I'm sorry, what was that?" I ask.

Becca smirks at me. "Helen was saying that she and her husband are from Cape Coral, Florida. Is that anywhere near you?"

I smile and launch myself into the discussion about Florida with Helen and the other guests, determined to put Jackson out of my mind.

AS WE'RE GETTING READY for bed that night, Becca side-eyes me while I massage cleanser onto my face.

"What?" I ask, rubbing circles on my chin.

She spits her toothpaste out into the sink and pins me with a knowing look. "Do you want to talk about your crush on Jackson?"

I bend over the sink to rinse my face, using the action as a way to delay my response.

After splashing water over my face a few more times than is strictly necessary, I straighten back up, and Becca hands me a towel. I pat my face dry.

"What crush on Jackson?" I finally respond.

"All that time you took to answer, and you still decided to go with denial?" She clucks her tongue. "Disappointing."

I sigh. "Fine. He's cute."

Becca's eyes light up. "I knew it! And I think he likes you, too."

I pause on my way out of the bathroom. *Really?* I quickly dismiss the idea. Jackson has been so hot and cold with me that it's hard to believe he might be thinking of me the way I'm thinking of him.

I snuggle into bed under the covers while Becca finishes up in the bathroom. She comes out and turns off the lights before getting into her own bed.

"I don't think Jackson likes me," I finally say. I'm lying on my back, staring toward the ceiling as my eyes adjust to the low light.

From the bed across from me, I hear Becca chuckle. "Believe me. I worked with Jackson all last summer, remember? He likes you."

I should drop the subject. Pretend to be asleep. Something. But my curiosity gets the better of me. "Did he date anyone at the ranch last summer?"

"No one. Not even a rumor of a hookup."

Hookup? I curl my fingers into fists and close my eyes. My heart pulses loudly enough for me to hear it, to feel it in my throat.

I'm way out of my depth here. Of course, it makes sense that at a ranch cut off from internet and TV, the staff of early twenty-somethings would be hooking up. I saw the same culture over the last four years at college, but I've never even—

"I've never kissed anyone," I blurt. Squeezing my eyes shut, I wait for Becca's response.

Jackson wasn't wrong at the gas station when he called me naive. I don't understand most of the crude jokes my friends make, and I'm not experienced with the complicated games men and women play when they're attracted to each other.

When I was growing up, all my friends were into horses or manatees or unicorns, and I fit in because I was interested in two things: horses and drawing horses. Then it was like one day, I looked up from my horse drawings to find that my friends had changed. All they talked about was makeup, skin care, accessorizing outfits, and boys. But I didn't care about any of that.

While makeup and clothes are still not on my list of priorities, I did eventually come around on boys. By then, though, it was like I was too late. I had missed something, some crucial lesson about how girls and boys were supposed to interact. I was friends with them and had embarrassing unreciprocated crushes, but none really expressed interest in me until college. Even then, the dates would leave me feeling unsatisfied, like something didn't quite fit.

"Never?" Becca finally asks. "Not even, like, a boy on the playground in elementary school?"

I prop myself up on my elbow and stare at Becca in her bed. "Were boys in your elementary school running around kissing people on the playground?"

Becca sits up on her bed and shrugs. "Yeah, a few. Weren't they at yours?"

"No!" I exclaim, but then I think about it. "To tell you the truth, they might have been, and I didn't notice."

"You've never kissed *anyone*?" Becca repeats. Between the distance and the darkness, I can't see her expression, but I can hear the bewilderment in the pitch of her voice.

"Never," I confirm. "It's not like I never wanted to or that I'm waiting on purpose. The circumstances haven't been right, I guess."

"Would you want Jackson to kiss you?"

Yes. The thought is immediate, instinctive. The conviction of it is what has my face burning, glad Becca can't see me from her bed.

"I don't know. Maybe," I answer out loud. "If he wanted to and the conditions were right."

"Hmm," Becca muses. "Jackson's a really nice guy, and obviously handsome. He would be a fantastic first kiss."

"You may think so, but that doesn't mean he wants to. He's probably not interested in me like that."

"He does, and he is."

"You sound so confident," I tease. Underneath my lighthearted veneer, though, I'm dying. Wistfulness, anticipation, hope. Fear. All warring with each other right behind my rib cage.

"I'm confident there's *something* there between you two. I would let it play out, if I were you."

"We'll see," I respond. There's no sense getting my hopes up, and all this talk about kissing Jackson is certainly not helping me keep my crush under control.

Becca lies back down and yawns.

"Please don't tell anyone else about how . . . how inexperienced I am." I drop my head back down on my pillow, finding the ceiling again.

"Of course not." She sounds annoyed, like she can't believe I would suggest such a thing. "What we say in our cabin stays in our cabin. Right?"

"Right," I agree right before the long, busy day catches up to me, and I drift off to sleep.

THE REST OF THE week passes without much interaction between Jackson and me, so I don't have an opportunity to test Becca's theory about his interest. Though, if he were interested, wouldn't he find excuses to talk to me? That's a thing, right?

I'm off again the following Sunday as a new crowd of guests arrive. After dinner, Leanne catches me before I escape back to my cabin.

"Dennis and I were talking about the schedule this week, and we're thinking of making a couple of changes."

I nod for her to continue, wondering what changes they discussed.

"I know Wednesday is supposed to be your second day off this week, but a little birdie told me that you haven't been to Yellowstone yet." She smiles, waiting for my confirmation.

"That's true," I say. I've wanted to explore Yellowstone from the minute I got the job at B&B. I've heard it's beautiful. "But I don't have my own vehicle here, so I'll have to wait until I'm off on a day I can borrow one of the ranch vans."

Leanne's smile grows wider. "*Or* we can switch your days off this week, and you can go with the group on Wednesday. Officially, you'll be a backup for one of the guides, but really he doesn't need much help, so you'll be free to enjoy yourself."

"Who's the guide?" I ask, my stomach fluttering because I think I already know.

"Danny, Nick, and Jackson are all driving vans to the park this week, but we'll put you with Jackson. He's the best."

I know she means the best Yellowstone guide, but I suspect we could put any number of other words behind that superlative and still be right.

The Yellowstone trip for the guests on Wednesdays is a driving tour with stops at the major sites. The outing lasts most of the day because the park is so large and takes so much time to travel through. It's a lot of togetherness, and I'm already anticipating the time I'll have with Jackson as we're confined to the van.

I'm letting things play out, like Becca suggested, but this opportunity feels like a gift.

Chapter Eleven

Jackson

WEDNESDAYS ARE YELLOWSTONE FIELD trip days, one of my favorite activities to lead for guests. I love seeing the look of awe on their faces as they experience the national park for the first time. Even taking this trip once a week for the last three summers, it doesn't get old. No two drives through the park are the same. I never know what animals we might spot or what questions my group might ask.

I've gotten pretty good at playing tour guide at Yellowstone National Park over the years, at least for the lower loop, which is the section of the enormous park that's reachable in a day trip from the ranch.

This week's guests are split between three vans. Nick's driving one of them. Danny's in charge of another, though it's his first time leading the tour, so Dennis sits shotgun to supervise and help him out.

I'm the lead van. The other two will follow me, especially for any unplanned stops to see wildlife. It also means I'm in charge of keeping us all on schedule. I can't help any delays from traffic in the park, but ultimately, we have to get the guests back to B&B in time for a late dinner.

Cell phones don't work in most places in the park, so each van has a walkie-talkie for us to communicate with each other.

I slide into the driver's seat of my assigned van, waiting out the flurry of activity and conversation as the guests divide themselves between the three vehicles.

I fiddle with my phone to get a downloaded playlist ready to go. George likes us to play country music when we're transporting guests—he says it adds to their cowboy experience. I find the list at the same time a knock on my window makes me jump.

I roll down the window. "What's up, Dennis?"

"I forgot to mention that we're bringing an extra staff member with us today. It's a big group, so we figured we'd need extra help. She's riding with you."

"No problem. It'll be good to have an extra set of hands." I don't think we'll need another staff member to help today, especially since we already have Dennis along to back up Danny. But Dennis is the boss.

Wait. Did he say "she"? I'm about to ask Dennis who the staff member is when he gives me a thumbs-up and walks back to Danny's van.

It's odd they wouldn't send the fourth activity guide, Jake, with us. Although, I think one couple staying behind today wanted to do some archery, so Jake is likely covering there. Probably one of the cabin wranglers then.

I focus on my task as passengers start loading into the back seats. A few taps on my phone screen and the twangy music starts rumbling through the van speakers.

As I adjust the volume, the front passenger-side door opens with a creak. Taylor climbs in and settles herself into the seat next to mine, a single center console between us.

My hand falters on the volume knob, but I play it cool.

"Did you draw the short straw?" I ask, mindful of keeping my smile friendly instead of eager.

She blinks at me. "Short straw?"

"For coming with us today. I figured they'd send a cabin wrangler."

Understanding lights up her expression. "Oh! No, I actually really wanted to come. I've never been to Yellowstone. Leanne wanted me to have the chance."

Ah, okay. Dennis doesn't actually think we need an additional staff member today. They do this sometimes for staff members who want to experience the park.

Still, I need to make sure I stay professional with Taylor today, no matter how much I feel the pull between us. My focus needs to be on the guests and giving them the best Yellowstone tour they can have.

"Everyone buckled?" I call over my shoulder. I hear mumbled assents, so I figure we're good to go. "Let's get rolling."

The East Gate entrance to Yellowstone National Park is a few miles west of the ranch, and so is our first stop of the day. I pull over onto the shoulder before we reach the entrance station, noting Nick and Danny stopping their vans behind me.

Directly in front of us is the giant wooden Yellowstone National Park sign, perfect for tourists posing for photos.

My passengers clamber out of the van to wait their turn with the sign. A family, whose minivan is parked in front of our line of ranch vans, poses themselves next to the National Park Service seal. The mom holds a squirming toddler as the dad stretches his arm, trying to capture the sign and his wife and three kids in one frame.

I jog over and hold out my hand. "Want me to get that for you?"

The mom gives me a look of exhausted relief. "Thanks," she says as her husband hands me the phone.

I snap a few shots, and I think I even manage to get a couple where all the kids are looking, if not smiling.

I give the dad back his phone with a smile and tip of my ball cap. "Enjoy the park," I tell them.

Our group is up next, so I remain in my spot to juggle phones and take pictures for the B&B Ranch guests.

When the guests finish, Taylor hands me her phone with a shy smile. She stands in front of the sign with her arms outstretched in an exuberant pose.

After I take a few pictures, I return her phone, and she takes it from me with a sheepish expression. "It's probably silly to want a picture with the sign, huh? Cliché."

I shake my head. "It's not silly if it makes you happy."

Her eyes—a brown that reminds me of varnished sandstone—sparkle in response.

Once everyone finishes their photos, we walk back to the vans. Taylor's up ahead of me, chatting with the guests. Not that I'm keeping track of her.

Nick appears at my side. "You've got a hitchhiker today, huh?" he asks in a low voice so only I can hear him.

I glare at him. "Worry about your own van."

He laughs. "Well, that's not nearly as much fun." He slaps me on the back as we reach my van. "See you at the next stop, Romeo."

I scowl at his retreating form. His voice was a little too loud there for my liking. Nick needs to learn to mind his own business.

It's a short drive from the sign to the park entrance. As we approach, Nick's teasing has already rolled off my back. I grin as I spot our first wildlife sighting of the day.

"Take a look to the right, everyone," I call over my shoulder. "Mama and baby bison."

Taylor gasps from the passenger seat as she watches the animals.

"This time of year, around late April through early June, is red-dog season at Yellowstone. That's what we call the baby bison because of their size and the color of their fur."

"It's so adorable!" one of my passengers says.

"So cute!" Taylor agrees.

This is one of my favorite parts of this job. When tourists—or really anyone who hasn't been to Yellowstone before—marvel at the animals roaming wild in their natural habitats, it changes their perception of freedom. When they look in awe at the natural wonders throughout the park, after being accustomed to seeing nothing but cities or suburbs at home, it changes their idea of beauty. I love seeing those moments.

I stop at the entrance and pay the admission fees for all three B&B vans.

Our first stop inside the park is the Lake Butte Overlook, about a thirty-minute drive from the entrance. It overlooks the massive Yellowstone Lake.

As we drive there, I tell the group more about the lake, like that it sits over a volcanic crater formed by past eruptions of the Yellowstone super volcano. The hydrothermal features in the area, like the hot springs and geysers, vent underground pressure and show that the volcano is still active.

I pull the van into a parking spot at the overlook. Everyone tumbles out, beelining toward the edge of the drop-off, with its panoramic views. The wide, placid lake and snowcapped peaks in the distance.

I inch up until I'm next to Taylor, blatantly ignoring Nick's all-too-knowing observation.

"This is dazzling," she breathes out, keeping her focus on the lake.

I hide a smile. If she's impressed with this view, the other sights we'll see today will absolutely blow her mind.

Lake Yellowstone is beautiful, don't get me wrong, but it's not even close to being my favorite spot in the park.

"We have a lot more to see today. Get your pictures here but make sure you leave room in your phone's memory for everything else, too." I throw her a wink that I don't think she sees because she still hasn't looked away from the vision in front of us.

I'm finding it difficult to look away, too, but it's not the lake that has my attention.

OUR NEXT STOP IS Old Faithful, the well-known geyser in Yellowstone. It got its name because it erupts predictably about every ninety minutes. Old Faithful has become one of the hot tourist spots in the park—people know when to arrive to see the show.

To cater to the tourists, Old Faithful Inn was built in the early 1900s. It's a seven-story building made out of logs with restaurants, shops, and hundreds of guest rooms. This is where we stop to have lunch before watching the geyser erupt.

The ranch chef, Chip, and his assistant, Lisa, packed us all lunch before we left this morning. Deli meat sandwiches with chips, apples, and cookies.

After parking the vans, Danny, Dennis, and I pull the coolers from the trunk and carry them upstairs to a balcony at the inn that overlooks Old Faithful. The balcony has picnic tables on the end farthest from the geyser and rows of wooden benches on the side that faces it.

We have thirty minutes until the next eruption, so we gather at the picnic tables to eat our lunch. I find myself seated next to Taylor again.

I swear I'm not doing it on purpose, but I wonder if she is. Again, the memory of the sparks between us the day we spent in Cody together that first week—and then again while white water rafting—floats to the top of my mind. She felt them, too, right?

She hasn't done anything overt to indicate she thinks of me as anything more than a coworker, or at most a friend, but maybe I should talk to her anyway. Let her know I'm not open to dating or a relationship or anything. Then she'll know where I stand, and I won't risk unintentionally leading her on.

On the other hand, we still have several more hours in the van together this afternoon, so I should probably wait so things don't become awkward between us.

Taylor's voice breaks through my musings. "You look deep in thought." Her lips are turned up in an adorable smile, a smudge of mustard on her cheek.

I clear my throat and return the smile. "Not at all."

Before I think it through, I take a clean napkin from my lunch bag and skim it over the smudge on her cheek. I feel the warmth of her skin through the thin paper, and my hand freezes.

Her eyes go wide, and I realize I've done the opposite of what I intended. I don't want to lead her on, but now I'm wiping mustard from her face?

Not my place. Not my place at all.

"Sorry," I mutter, dropping my hand. "You had some mustard."

She blushes, her cheeks turning a sweet pink in lovely contrast with her dark eyelashes. She grabs up her own napkin and swipes at her face.

I clear my throat again. "You got it."

Neither of us says anything else. So much for not making things awkward.

Finally, Taylor tries again. "Seeing Old Faithful will be cool. I've always heard about it. Of course, you must have seen it a bunch of times by now."

I stop myself before I clear my throat a third time, cursing my nervous tic. Instead, I open my mouth to respond, hoping my voice sounds normal. "Yeah, every week for the past three summers. It is cool, but not my favorite thing in the park. Old Faithful is a little too touristy for me."

"What is your favorite thing?"

"Mount Washburn," I answer. "It's not one of the stops for the guest tour, but I like to hike up on my days off sometimes. The views are amazing."

She frowns. "What about your favorite thing on the guest tour?"

I need to consider this question. "Maybe Grand Prismatic Spring? That's where we're headed next. Or the Dragon's Mouth Spring is very cool. It's one of our last stops." I roll through the various sights we'll see today and smile. "I have a good idea what your favorite spot will be."

Her eyes light up. "What?"

But I don't want to spoil the surprise. "You'll see."

Chapter Twelve

Taylor

WATCHING OLD FAITHFUL ERUPT, spraying water more than one hundred feet in the air, is impressive. I can see what Jackson means about it being touristy, though. We crowd in with hundreds of other people, jostling for a vantage point on the viewing platform.

It's more people than I've been around at one time since I arrived in Wyoming, and I feel strangely stifled after weeks of nothing but open space.

After the geyser calms down, we're back in the van. As we rumble past rocks and trees with a river flowing along with us on our left, I try to make sense of the man sitting next to me.

Jackson is open and friendly, like when he jumped in to help strangers with their photo by the Yellowstone sign earlier. But at times, he's distant and almost dismissive.

The mixed signals I'm getting from him make my heart spin. He says I'm pretty. He wipes mustard from my cheek—oh my gosh, SO embarrassing—but he's also apt to avoid me, looking annoyed when I sit down next to him.

I'm not sure what to think.

Fortunately, like I told Grammy, I'm not here for a romance. I look out my window at the mountains rolling past. I'm here for *this*. I'm here for adventure and trying things I've never done before and seeing and doing amazing bucket list items.

We drive fifteen minutes to another crowded parking lot. As Jackson parks the van, I see a boardwalk and clouds of steam floating in the air through the windshield.

"Where are we now?" I ask.

"Grand Prismatic Spring," Jackson answers, shifting the van into park.

One of his favorites, I remember.

We have springs in Florida. Lots of them. The water stays at a constant temperature year-round. In the summer a natural spring is a delightful place to cool off from the hot, sticky weather, and in the winter, the spring waters are where manatees gather to stay warm. The water is clear and beautiful.

I wonder what a Yellowstone spring is like. The floating steam and Jackson's earlier words about the hydrothermal features of the park make me think this spring is different from what I'm used to back home. *Like almost everything else I've experienced here so far.*

Jackson claps his hands and gets the group's attention as they file out of the van. "Okay, everyone, we'll be here for about twenty minutes. Stay on the boardwalks and meet back here if you get separated from the group." He points behind us. "There is a public restroom here if you need it before we continue. It's an hour to our next stop."

When the last person in the group is out of the van and walking toward the spring, Jackson grabs my wrist and tugs me along. "Come on, this is really cool."

I stare at his fingers curled around my arm, surprised at the electricity of his warm skin against mine. When Jackson notices he's still holding on, he lets go. He doesn't apologize or say anything about it, just drops his hand and continues on the path with me trailing behind him. *More mixed signals*. But it doesn't matter. I'm not here for him.

The first thing I see, off to the left, is a shallow pond of water with clouds of steam billowing up.

"This is the Excelsior Geyser Crater," Jackson says loud enough for the members of our group in front of us to hear. "It pumps superheated water from below ground into the Firehole River. The steam is from the hot water cooling when it reaches the surface."

One of our guests calls out, "What's the white crusty stuff on the ground?"

"Siliceous sinter. The hot water from underground carries dissolved silica—silicon mixed with oxygen—but as the water cools, it can't hold the silica anymore, so it gets deposited on the ground and forms a hard mineral crust."

After pausing for a few minutes to take pictures of the crater, we continue following the boardwalk. It forks off in two directions, a loop that will take us past Grand Prismatic Spring. We keep to the left along with the other tourists heading toward the spring.

As we get closer to the spring, the wind picks up, blowing steam into our faces along with a strong sulfur smell mixed with something gamey.

Soon, we stand in front of a kind of beach, the ground glassy and reflecting the sky above. Beyond that, a pool of deep blue water, the steam coming off it so heavily I can hardly see the surface.

I've never seen anything like this. I've never been anywhere like this. Any thoughts of Jackson or romance fade away, and instead, I'm noticing everything about the scene in front of me. The green trees on the hills in the distance. The ground next to the boardwalk that looks like hardened mud, cracks and ridges running across it in a chaos of pattern.

Nature takes so many forms, and I realize how limited my worldview has been. What other wonders are out there for me to see outside of a painting or photograph?

As I'm marveling, I notice some sort of dark lump out in the water. The steam is thick, so even when I squint to get a better look, I still can't quite tell what it is.

"Grand Prismatic Spring is the largest hot spring in the United States," Jackson recites. "From above, its namesake is more obvious, but you can see from here the bright colors, like a prism. Blue, yellow, orange, red, and green."

A woman nudges her son, who looks to be maybe nine years old. "Go ahead and ask," she encourages.

The boy raises his hand timidly.

Jackson grins and points to him. "What's up?"

"How hot is it?" the boy asks.

Jackson bends down so he's at eye level with the boy. "160 degrees. You definitely wouldn't want to take a bath in that water."

The boy wrinkles his nose. "I don't want to take a bath at all."

Jackson widens his eyes in a playful expression and takes an exaggerated step backward. "Noted." He waves a hand in front of his nose. "I was wondering what that smell is."

The boy giggles, his face turning red, and puts his hands on his hips. "That's not me!"

Jackson raises his eyebrows in feigned disbelief. "Uh-huh."

I bite back a smile at the cute exchange. Jackson's good with kids. It's not the first time I've noticed. He always makes sure to include kids in conversations at meals and listens to them as they share their excitement over the activities they're planning to do. He's patient and encouraging while he's teaching them how to shoot an arrow at the archery range.

Knowing this about him does nothing to help curb my feelings, which are already expanding beyond the boundaries of "crush" territory at an alarming pace. But maybe it's not a bad thing to lean into this attraction, especially if he's feeling it, too.

We walk farther along the boardwalk to where a park ranger is posted answering questions. Behind her, out in the water, is the large dark lump. As I listen to the questions and answers between the visitors and the ranger, I realize that the lump out in the water is a bison.

"It stumbled out here overnight earlier in the week," the ranger explains. "It likely died within minutes due to the extreme temperature of the water."

"Explains the smell," one visitor comments.

The ranger nods. "Yes. Usually, the sulfur smell is much more pronounced, but today what you're smelling is essentially cooked bison." She shrugs, like it's no big deal that nature can be so gruesome.

And it *is* fascinating, in a grim sort of way.

I've fallen behind the rest of the group, so I leave the ranger and her Q&A session and follow the boardwalk the rest of the way around, looping back toward the parking lot.

When everyone's in the van, Jackson drives us back to the main road to continue following the lower loop.

"This next stretch of the drive will take around an hour," he reminds us. "There's nice scenery, as there is everywhere in the park, but feel free to rest if you need to."

Shuffling and murmuring from the back seats indicate that the guests are getting comfortable for this next leg of the tour. One little boy, around ten years old, focuses his attention out the window, his Yellowstone junior ranger booklet in hand. One of the activities is to mark off the kinds of wildlife in the park as you see them, and he has been adamant in his goal to see them all.

Behind him, his younger sister lays her head against her dad's shoulder and closes her eyes. I'm tempted to rest for a bit, too, but I also don't want to squander this opportunity to get to know Jackson better.

"What's our next stop?" I ask.

"The Grand Canyon of the Yellowstone," he says without elaborating.

"Can you tell me about it?" I prompt.

Jackson twists his neck to look at me, a crooked smile on his lips. "I don't want to spoil anything, but I think you'll really like it."

My heart flip-flops inside my chest at the thought of Jackson taking any time to consider what I'd like.

Chapter Thirteen

Taylor

The conversation stalls. If he doesn't want to talk about the park, I'll go in a different direction.

"Tell me more about rock climbing. You said you have a big trip planned at the end of the summer?"

His expression brightens. "Yeah, Gannett Peak. It's on the other side of the mountains from where we are now. About a six-hour drive to go around them. It's the highest point in Wyoming, but it's hard to get to."

"How do you get there?"

A smile stretches across his face. "A twenty-mile hike that includes crossing glaciers."

"Twenty miles!" Before even getting to the mountain he wants to climb? I'm exhausted thinking about it.

"Yep, carrying a fifty-pound pack of supplies and gear."

"Are you going by yourself?" Because that sounds really dangerous.

"No, with a guided group. We're going in August, right as the last week at B&B Ranch finishes up. We'll take two days to hike in, one day to summit, and two days to hike back out."

I'm honestly appalled. Why in the world does that sound fun to anyone? "How do you even prepare for a trip like that?"

Keeping his eyes on the road, Jackson shrugs. "Well, I told you about climbing the frozen waterfalls. That was good training. I've been using my days off this summer to do some of the climbs around here—Shoshone Canyon, the North Fork, Cedar Mountain, Beartooth Pass—to keep my skills sharp, especially on snow and ice. I've also been doing frequent heavy pack training. Elk Mountain and Heart Mountain are great for that. The ranch is the perfect place for me to be this summer because we're close to so many great climbs and trails."

I whoosh out a breath. "Sounds intense."

He glances at me. "It is, but I didn't wake up one day and climb a frozen waterfall, you know. I worked up to it. It started when I was a teenager doing indoor rock climbing. Then after I built up my skills, I got into some of the beginner climbs around Boulder with my friends. The Flatirons, BoCan. Everything spiraled from there, especially after—" He breaks off, his jaw tightening. "Especially around my senior year of high school."

That pause. What is he not saying? Despite Jackson's confusing mixed signals, I find him fascinating. His good looks don't hurt, of course, but it's more about the layers I suspect are buried under his cheerful-ambassador veneer.

He knows grief. He holds people at arm's length but is excellent at doing it without the person noticing. I notice.

He clears his throat. "But what about you? I know you grew up on a horse farm, but did you have a pony instead of a baby stroller, or was it more gradual than that?"

I smile. "No, that was about it. I don't remember my first ride because I was so young. I've seen pictures, though. I've been around horses so long that loving them isn't a question. Do I love breathing? Same thing."

At one point, I considered whether I would take over Steed Farm when my parents retired. I'm their only child, and it is a family business. Though it would solve my what-am-I-doing-with-my-life dilemma, taking over the farm feels like the safe option. I'm not sure it's what I want—settling into the same life I've always had.

I'm not saying I need to climb mountains like my thrill-seeking coworker, but I'd like to experience . . . I don't know . . . more than what I already know. It's why I'm in Wyoming. Well, that and post-Christmas desperation.

"What about painting, then? How did you get into that?" Jackson presses.

I chuckle. This I have a story for. "Ms. Daniels," I say. "Second grade. We were learning about dinosaurs in science, and she gave us a coloring page with a *Brontosaurus* on it. The other kids colored their dinosaurs with earth tones like brown and dark green, but I wanted my *Brontosaurus* to be beautiful. I think I used every color in the crayon box. My classmates laughed at me, but Ms. Daniels defended me. She said that we don't really know what color dinosaur skin was because we only have fossils. Maybe they were colorful."

"That was nice of her."

"It was, and it inspired me to start drawing everything I saw in the way I wanted it to be rather than focusing on how it really was. I got my first set of watercolors when I was ten, and painting has been my medium of choice ever since."

As I finish the story, Jackson turns into a driveway with a sign that says "Artist Point Parking Lot."

He stops the van, turning to me as he shifts into park. He slides his sunglasses to the top of his head and grins. His eyes are a warm, earthy brown in the afternoon sunlight. I imagine the blobs of yellow and purple I'd mix to produce the shade.

"Have you ever seen something so naturally beautiful that you didn't need to paint it differently? Something where the reality lived up to your imagination?"

His question surprises me, but not more than my immediate thought in response: *You*. I blush and swat away the notion with an upturned hand. "Sure, but not often. I can always think of some way to improve a scene."

His grin widens. "Wait until you see this."

Jackson turns to address the guests. "Okay, everyone, wake up! We're here at Artist Point. There's a trail to the lookout point and then make your way back here to the van when you're done. This is a spectacular view of the Grand Canyon of the Yellowstone, including the Lower Falls. Have your cameras ready!"

I'm leery of how much Jackson is building this up. We've already seen some sublime sights today. Is this really going to be so much more impressive?

As the guests make their way to the lookout, Jackson and I trail behind them. In a voice just loud enough for me to hear, he tells a story about what we're about to see.

"An artist named Thomas Moran participated in a trip to survey the land here in the 1870s. From the spot we're heading to right now, Moran sketched different views of the Grand Canyon of the Yellowstone. One of those became an oil painting that helped convince Congress to pass the Yellowstone National Park Bill of 1871 that designated this land as a reserved public park, and was the start of the national parks system. Congress later bought the painting for ten thousand dollars, and it was on display in the Capitol for many years."

I peer over at him. "Is that all true?"

He chuckles. "More or less. What's one hundred percent true is that Thomas Moran's artwork of Yellowstone helped convince Congress to preserve this land."

It's an impressive story. An example of how art can influence politics and ecology. How beauty can inspire change in the real world. I'm all the more eager to see the view from that lookout ahead. "The power of art."

"The power of art," he agrees.

Finally, we reach the lookout, a small platform surrounded by cement walls about chest high. I try to look around but can't get more than a glimpse through the crowd of tourists. Jackson puts his hands on my shoulders and guides me to the wall looking east.

I gasp. The colors catch my attention first. Tall, rugged walls of yellow and peach rock, capped with deep-green trees like frosting on top of a slice of cake. I can barely make out a river at the base of the canyon, white water rushing through the gorge.

Again, I'm mixing paint in my mind's eye. How much red would I add to match the salmon-colored tint down the canyon walls? What combination of blue and white would capture that gorgeous sky?

"You can see how this park got the name Yellowstone," Jackson murmurs next to my ear, his hands still on my shoulders.

I hum, imagining swiping my brush against the canvas to recreate the stunning landscape in front of me.

"It's beautiful," I say.

"You think so?" A layer of smugness in his voice draws my eyes over my shoulder to his face. He's smirking, his expression mischievous.

Steering me by the shoulders, he leads me through and around groups of people to the westerly wall. "What about this?"

My gasp is sharper this time, an involuntary gust of air expelled from my lungs that leaves me breathless. Words have no meaning. All my focus and energy center around two points on my body. The spot on my shoulder where Jackson's hand is warm and firm through my shirt and jacket. And my eyes, which are gobbling up the scenery like a baby with its first birthday cake, smearing and fisting, anything to get more of it into my body.

In front of me, a postcard. A painting in perfectly mixed oils. The rugged yellow canyon walls, the earthy tree line at the top of the gorge, but also, a waterfall in the distance, churning white water into the cool blue-green river, the finest mist floating ethereally up from the base.

If the eastern view is exquisite, the western is a masterpiece.

I wish I had my good camera.

I make do with my phone, snapping shots from several angles. Usually, I paint from photographs, so I need enough of them so that I can reassemble this view in my mind and then on the canvas.

No question that I will paint this.

I move back to the eastern wall and take photos from that vantage point as well.

Until I hear Jackson's soft chuckle next to my ear, I forget he's next to me, forget anyone is here other than me and the beauty around me.

In my surprise, I lose my balance. Before I can fall, Jackson's arms are around my waist, holding me up. My racing heart could be because I almost wound up face-first on the concrete or because of the strength and steadiness of the man whose hands are resting on my hips. My stumble turned me toward him, and now our chests are close enough together that the metal button on my jacket scrapes against the zipper on his, producing a confusingly satisfying sound I know I'll be replaying the rest of the day.

"Careful," Jackson rasps, a puff of air from his mouth tickling my lips.

I tilt my chin up until our eyes are level. His are fire, the purple undertones I noticed earlier deepening into a flame that threatens to incinerate me. What little air there is between us is heavy, charged and broiling despite the chilly weather.

Is Jackson going to kiss me? Do I want him to? It would be my first kiss, and I can't think of a more strikingly romantic backdrop. What a memory it would make.

The moment dissolves as quickly as it solidified when we hear commotion behind us. Jackson makes sure I'm steady on my feet and drags his hands away.

I turn toward the hubbub to see flashes of images through the crowd: a man down on one knee, the fabric of his jeans darkening where it meets the damp ground. He holds a small box in one upturned hand. In front of him stands a woman bundled in a blush-pink puffer jacket with her hands pressed over her mouth.

We're too far from them to hear what they're saying, but it's clearly a proposal. The people pressed in around the couple start cheering and clapping, so I assume she's said yes.

The energy is contagious. I add my enthusiastic clapping to the round of applause as the man slips a ring on his new fiancée's finger and they embrace.

I sigh. I had been thinking how perfect a first kiss at Artist Point would be but imagine a proposal! I hope he had the foresight to hire a photographer to immortalize the moment in front of that gorgeous backdrop.

Jackson tugs on the sleeve of my jacket. "We better get back to the van. I think most of our guests have headed down already."

I nod and follow him wordlessly back down the path to the parking lot, casting one last look over my shoulder at my new favorite landscape.

When I turn again, Jackson's smiling, paused on the walkway waiting for me. "I knew you'd love it."

My stomach flutters, and as much as I do love Artist Point, I think I would have loved it a little bit more if Jackson had kissed me here.

Chapter Fourteen

Jackson

THE REST OF THE Yellowstone trip goes as planned. We drive through Hayden Valley and pull over to see herds of bison. We stop at the Mud Volcano and see one of my favorite sites, the Dragon's Mouth Spring. On the way out, we spend a few minutes in the gift shop at Fishing Bridge.

Through it all, I can't stop thinking about Taylor. Of course, she's sitting right next to me, so it would be hard to avoid her in my thoughts anyway, but specifically, I can't stop thinking about that moment at Artist Point.

If we hadn't been interrupted by that proposal . . .

Well, we were interrupted, so who's to say what might have happened. Plus, we were on the clock, some of our guests likely still lingering at the overlook, so it would have been entirely inappropriate. It's good nothing happened, but I can't deny that I really wanted it to. And that's the piece of all this that's been on my mind nonstop.

I can talk to her and see how she's feeling. Maybe she could be on the same page as I am, could be interested in seeing where things go this summer.

We're back at the ranch in time for a late dinner. Afterward, most of the guests and many of the employees settle into the saloon for games and conversation. None of us who went on the Yellowstone trip today are on duty tonight, so when I see Taylor duck out the dining room doors, I follow.

I catch her halfway up the path to our cabins.

"Taylor," I call.

She spins around and smiles at me, but her eyes are wild like she's looking for an escape.

"Hey."

I stop in front of her. "Hi."

Now that I'm committed to this conversation, I'm blanking on what to say. *Hey, you know how we almost kissed earlier? What was up with that, and would you want to try again?* Probably not the best approach. I clear my throat.

"Hi," I say again, and run my hand through my hair. "Can I talk to you?"

The spot between her eyebrows crinkles, and she raises a hand, palm up. "Sure?"

Laughter behind me has me turning my head to see Danny, Kyra, and Mia coming up the path. I frown.

"Not here." I take Taylor's hand and tug her in the direction of the creek. "Come on."

She follows me off the trail and behind the cabins. There's an alcove here, my own hidden spot where the shrubs clear by the creek. A rock with a flat top next to the water makes an ideal place to sit and relax. I come here often on my own—especially at night when I can't sleep—to let the sound of the creek soothe me.

Taylor sits on the rock and looks at me expectantly. I remain standing, flustered by the coming conversation and the unexpected way my heart stutters seeing Taylor here in my sacred space. I didn't plan to bring her here; it's where my feet took us without me thinking about it.

"So, about what happened earlier at Artist Point . . ." I trail off, unsure of what to say next.

Taylor dips her finger in the water and swirls it around, creating a tiny whirlpool. She watches the spinning water as she asks, "Were you going to kiss me?"

Okay, no beating around the bush here. Her forthright question helps me shore up my own courage. I take a breath and go for honesty.

"I wanted to, yeah." I swallow. "Would that have been okay?"

She looks up from the water and meets my eyes. "Yes," she whispers, but the tremor in her voice makes me wonder if she means it.

"What's wrong?"

Her cheeks flush, and she looks away again.

I take two steps back from the rock Taylor's sitting on. *Have I been reading this all wrong?* I could've sworn we had a mutual attraction going here, but if my attention isn't welcome, I'll leave her alone.

"Taylor," I start, my voice wobbly. I clear my throat and take another step back for good measure. "I'm sorry. I didn't mean to make you uncomfortable. I—"

"No, Jackson, I, um . . ." She jumps to her feet and loops her fingers around my wrist, pulling me closer. "There's nothing wrong, I just . . . Sorry. Give me a second."

She closes her eyes and inhales once, and then again. When she looks at me again, she's still blushing, but there's a determined glint in her expression. With her fingers still wrapped around my wrist, her voice is steady. "You should know that I . . . I've never kissed anyone before."

I reel back, and her fingers slide off my arm. *How is that possible?* Taylor—beautiful, vivacious, sweet Taylor—hasn't had her first kiss yet at twenty-two?

"Why?" I stammer.

Her face heats even more, turning red all the way to the tips of her ears. "It just kind of happened. Or didn't happen, I guess. I'm not purposely waiting or anything."

And then I'm stunned at how close *I* was to thoughtlessly kissing her earlier today. Taylor deserves an exceptional first-kiss experience. The perfect setting at the perfect well-thought-out moment with a guy who's perfect for her. The golden ratio of first kisses.

That guy's not me. Not when I'm climbing dangerous cliffs and flying a single-engine Cessna every weekend. Not when I live thousands of miles away from her home and family. Not when I can't promise her anything more than the summer.

What a poor choice I would be for Taylor's first kiss.

"Okay," Taylor says soothingly. "I can see that you're kind of freaking out." She pauses and when she speaks again, her tone is heated. "Which is insulting, honestly."

She puts her hands on her hips. "What, because I've never kissed anyone, you assume I'm not worth kissing?" Poking a finger into my chest, she continues, "I'd be an amazing kisser!"

I watch her lips form into an indignant pout, and I have no doubt that kissing her *would* be amazing. For me, anyway. But how would she feel about it, three months down the road, or a year from now when she barely remembers my name?

And yet, selfish guy that I am, I don't think I'm willing to walk away completely. Taylor entrances me like no one I've ever met before.

She pokes me in the chest again, and I cover her hand with mine, holding it in place. "I know."

Taylor stills, her nose scrunching adorably. "You're not insulting me?"

I lift my shoulders. "Not intentionally."

"Why are you freaking out, then?" She tries to pull her hand away, and I loosen my grip. Before letting her go completely, I rub my thumb in a circle against the skin on her inner wrist.

She shivers, and while I'd like to think it's because of my gesture, it could be because of the growing chill in the evening air.

"I'm sorry for freaking out. I wasn't expecting you to say that." I pause as I consider my next words. "Given this new information, I think it's best if we move forward slowly. If you want to move forward at all, that is."

She rubs her upper arms, eyes cutting through me. "Move forward with what, exactly?"

Good question. Before her revelation, I was ready to dive into kissing her, pursuing *something* with her without labels or promises. But that doesn't feel right anymore. I pegged it from the beginning. Taylor is not a situationship type of girl, and I am not a relationship type of guy, at least not with where I am in my life right now.

"A friendship?" I suggest, knowing full well the self-control it will take for me to stay in that zone.

She narrows her eyes, but not before I see a spark of disappointment flit through them.

Finally, she thrusts her hand toward me. "Friends," she agrees.

She intends for me to shake it, but I wrap her hand up in both of mine, sliding the pads of my fingers against her skin.

She pulls in a quiet breath but recovers quickly into a smirk. Instead of pulling away, she guides me back to the rock she was sitting on earlier and sits, tugging me down next to her.

"Okay, friend." She pats my thigh with her free hand. "Tell me about why you don't like horses."

Chapter Fifteen

Taylor

Jackson's face pales, and he clears his throat nervously. Though it's past eight o'clock at this point, the sun hasn't yet set, so I can see the series of emotions as they flash across his face in the still-lingering light. I can't identify them all—I don't know him nearly well enough for that. Yet.

How late the sun sets in Wyoming has been a strange and unexpected part of my adventure here. Even in summer in Florida, it's dark by nine. And when I've been getting up to tend to the horses at six in the morning, it's already light out. The nights are so short.

As Jackson continues to hesitate, I wait him out. I'm disappointed he's not going to kiss me, but I can still satisfy my curiosity about him in other ways. I find myself wanting to know all this man's secrets, which is additional proof that my crush is getting out of hand.

Finally, Jackson says, "It's a long story."

I place my hands behind me on the rock and lean back. "I've got time."

With a sigh, he fixes his gaze on the stream below us. "My . . . my mom loved horses. *Loved* them. We didn't have our own, but whenever she could, she would go riding at this stable outside of Boulder."

I note his use of the past tense, but I tuck the question away, not wanting to interrupt his story.

"When I was a kid, maybe eight or so, I begged and begged to go with her and try it. She finally scheduled a time to take me, but at the last minute, something came up—I don't remember what—and I got upset when she said we'd have to reschedule. She asked my dad to take me instead.

"We got to the stable, and I changed my mind right away when I saw the horses in person. They were humongous. But I had made such a big deal about going that I didn't want to say anything. So, I got on the horse, even though I was super anxious about it."

Uh-oh. I can already see where this is going. Horses are sensitive. They can easily pick up on the emotions of the person riding them. If they detect that their rider is scared, they think there must be something dangerous happening and become skittish, on high alert.

"At one point, I guess I pressed too tight with my legs, and the horse freaked out and threw me off. Only my dad saw what happened, and he brushed it off, telling me I was fine even though my arm really hurt. I wasn't supposed to say anything to my mom about it, he said.

"By the time my mom got home later that night, I was in so much pain that she could tell instantly that something was wrong. She got the whole story out of me in five minutes, and five minutes after that, we were on our way to the hospital. Turns out my arm was broken."

It's the longest speech I've ever heard Jackson give while talking about himself, but he isn't done yet. He swallows before continuing, his eyes so zoned in on the water in the creek that I'm not certain he remembers I'm here.

"It was the only time I ever saw my mom get angry—like burn-down-the-world, take-no-prisoners furious—and it was all directed at my dad. They didn't know I could hear them arguing after I went to bed that night. My dad said something about not being good under pressure, and my mom called him a coward."

Quietly, Jackson murmurs, "I guess the signs were there all along."

"What do you mean?" I ask.

He clears his throat then and sits up as if re-emerging into the present. He blinks at me but instead of answering my question says, "I've stayed away from horses ever since."

So many details in that story feel incomplete, but I don't press him further. Instead, I lift my hand to his shoulder and squeeze. "That must have been scary, especially for a kid."

I let the sentiment sit between us for several minutes as we each follow our own thoughts. Mine focus on how unfair it is to blame the horse for the fiasco and how much Jackson is missing out on by abandoning the idea of riding altogether.

Hesitantly, I say, "But . . ."

Jackson must see some of what I'm thinking reflected in my eyes because he scowls. "But?"

The corners of my lips quirk up. "*But*, you know what they say about falling off a horse."

He grimaces. "I think that advice works better metaphorically than literally."

I shake my head. "Nah. Every rider has fallen off a horse at some point or another. Granted, breaking a bone is more extreme, but still."

Jackson doesn't look convinced.

"Have you ever gotten hurt while rock climbing?" I ask.

He shifts his weight on our rock bench. "Well, yeah. Mostly scrapes and strained muscles. A buddy of mine tore his meniscus."

"But it's not exactly *safer* than riding horses, is it?" I prod. "It's maybe even *more* dangerous?"

He purses his lips, as if he's reluctant to concede the point. It gives me an idea.

I hold up a finger. "I have a deal for you. I am willing to do some *mild, beginner* mountain climbing with you . . ." Jackson's eyes light up like he's won a prize. "*If* you agree to come on a trail ride with me."

His expression dims at the second part of my offer. "I don't know."

I nudge his side. "Oh, come on! I'll even put you on our gentlest horse. The one we assign to seven-year-olds."

At this, he chuckles and raises his eyebrows. "Seven-year-olds?"

I grin. "Mm-hmm. You're at least as brave as a seven-year-old, aren't you?"

He sets his jaw. "I'm brave," he mutters with a playful pout.

I know he is, about everything I've seen from him so far *except* horses.

I face him fully and bring my hands to my hips. "Prove it."

He rolls his eyes. "Fine. Challenge accepted."

I pump my fist. "Yay! Oh, this will be so fun!"

He smiles at my enthusiasm, his eyes softening with a fondness I'm not sure how to interpret, especially considering our "friendship" conversation earlier.

We sit in companionable silence for a few minutes, until I break it with the question I've been dying to ask. "You talked about your mom in the past tense. Did she pass away?"

His expression clouds over, and he shakes his head. "No, ma'am. I've shared enough for one night." He nudges my boot with his sneaker. "Another time, maybe."

Fair enough. We've both shared some weighty things tonight. I can't expect to draw this man completely out of his shell in one conversation.

I yawn and rest my head against his shoulder. "I'll hold you to that."

I feel the rumble of laughter rolling through his chest. "I'm sure you will."

BECCA IS WAITING FOR me when Jackson walks me back to my cabin. Well, he's not really walking me back to my cabin as much as walking back to his next-door cabin at the same time as me.

She pounces as soon as I'm through the door. "What was that little rendezvous? Are you and Jackson . . ." She trails off, raising her eyebrows meaningfully.

I sigh. "No. But maybe yes? I don't know. We had a moment on the Yellowstone trip, but then I'm pretty sure he walked it back."

She squints at me. "What does that mean?"

I tell her the whole story of the almost-kiss at Artist Point and then our conversation by the creek. Not the part about his fear of horses, of course, but the first part, when I told him that I'd never been kissed and he freaked out and declared us just friends.

She folds her arms over her chest and scowls. "So, what, he only wants experienced women? What an idiot. I didn't think Jackson was like that."

I didn't either. But he did mention "taking things slow," so maybe he wants to be friends for now and eventually work up to more? How slow, though? Now that it's mid-June, we have less than two months of the summer left, and then I'll be going home to Florida to figure out my next steps, and he'll be off on his hike-slash-rock-climbing-challenge thing. Will I ever hear from him again after that?

I wave my hand dismissively. "No, it's fine. I'm not looking for any kind of summer romance, anyway. Friends works for me."

As I settle into bed, I can't stop thinking of the moment at Artist Point when he was about to kiss me and how badly I wanted that. But I also think about our conversation, how he opened up to me. How good that felt.

I glance out the cabin window from my bed. It's finally dark and the stars are out in full force. I'm much too old to wish on stars, but I find myself sending up a silent plea anyway. *Please, can't I have both?*

Chapter Sixteen

Jackson

My cabin is dark when I sneak inside and close the front door after saying good night to Taylor. I hope this means that Nick's still down at the lodge.

The thought has no sooner formed in my brain when the room illuminates, and I see Nick leaning on the wall near the light switch. His arms are crossed, and he has an annoying smirk on his face.

Of course I'm not that lucky.

"And where, pray tell, have you been?" He gives me a look like he's my dad and I'm a teenager out after curfew.

I've managed to avoid Nick's nosiness since we got back from Yellowstone, keeping Danny between us as a buffer through dinner until I could make my escape.

There's no telling what Nick might have seen at Artist Point. I wasn't exactly cognizant of my surroundings while Taylor was in my arms. I wasn't exactly aware of anything except the feel of her hips under my hands, her needy eyes, and her breath against my lips.

"Walking around," I tell Nick.

Seeing that I'm not going to spill, Nick tries a different tactic. "That proposal up at Artist Point today was something else, huh?"

So, he *was* still at the outlook when Taylor and I almost kissed. There's still a chance he didn't notice us, though.

I shrug noncommittally. "I guess."

I hang my jacket up on the coatrack near the door and step toward the bathroom. Nick moves to block my path.

"But maybe you were busy with something else? Or should I say *someone*?" He raises his eyebrows.

Busted. Still, there's nothing really to tell him. I'm not going to betray Taylor's confidence about the whole never-been-kissed thing, and the bottom line is that nothing happened. And nothing will.

"I didn't realize you were such a gossip, Davenport."

His eyebrows rise even higher. "Not gossiping, Hollis. Trying to support a friend."

I sigh and run my hand over my hair. "Well, there's no need. Nothing's happening. Nothing's going to happen."

Nick's expression wilts. "She's not interested?" His arms fall to his sides, and he steps out of my way. "Dang, I'm sorry, man. That's tough. I really thought she was into you."

How can I explain the situation to my well-meaning friend? *Should* I even explain it?

"I guess not," I hedge. Then some truth: "I'm not the right guy for her. We decided to be friends."

Nick cups his hand around his chin. "Friends, huh?" He mutters it again as he walks away. "I can work with friends."

MY NEXT DAY OFF is Saturday, and I have some tentative plans for another solo climb, though I'm anxious to cash in on my agreement with Taylor to take her "mountain climbing."

I'm not going to take her mountain climbing for real; the idea that I have percolating is more of a hike than a climb. I put the second part of the deal—a trail ride where I'll need to ride a horse—out of my mind.

Best not to dwell on it.

I walk to breakfast with Nick, who also has the day off, and he seems worryingly upbeat, even for him.

"You have plans today?" he asks.

"Yeah, I was thinking I'd head over to the Island for a climb."

Nick bobs his head. "You *could* do that."

I glance warily at my friend and roommate. "But?"

"But Becca and Taylor are off today, too, and I kind of told them we'd take them fly-fishing."

I stop walking. "Without checking with me?"

On the one hand, I'm annoyed about whatever Nick is scheming, but on the other hand, I can't stop the thrill of anticipation I feel at spending time with Taylor, even if it is under Nick's watchful eye.

"I know. I'm sorry. I'm sure it will be awkward after she rejected you earlier this week."

I clench my teeth to hold back the words my pride would have me blurt out. *She didn't reject me. I did it for her.*

I catch up with Nick, and we continue down the path together.

"But," Nick continues, "maybe if she spends more time with you, she'll realize you *are* right for her."

Before I can protest, we climb the stairs up to the front porch of the lodge and find Taylor and Becca waiting for us.

Becca skips over first. "We're so excited to go fly-fishing today!"

I shoot a murderous look at my roommate, who grins and points toward the office. "I'm going to get our fishing licenses squared away."

Taylor inches up, smiling shyly. We ended Wednesday night on friendly terms, and though I didn't give her the good night kiss she wanted, I did fork over some of my emotional baggage, so that has to count for something.

"It's something I've been wanting to try," Taylor says, giving me a look like *Is this okay?*

My annoyance with Nick springing this outing on me melts away.

If Taylor wants to go fishing, I'll take her fishing.

I smile wide enough to encompass both women. "We're excited too. There's almost nothing better than standing in the cool water of the Shoshone on a warm summer day." I focus on Taylor's face. "An experience to remember, for sure."

Becca grabs Taylor's hand. "I got to go once last summer, and it was so relaxing! I didn't even care that I didn't catch any fish."

Taylor, her eyes bright, tugs Becca toward the dining room. "Let's eat so we can get to the river!"

I can't help but chuckle as the two friends disappear through the doors to the lodge. So much for training today. Looks like I'm going fishing instead.

AFTER A QUICK BREAKFAST where we make plans with Becca and Taylor to meet them by the fishing shed at nine, Nick and I get all the gear ready to go.

George and Pamela are great about letting staff use the ranch equipment when they don't need it for guests. As long as we clean everything when we get back to make sure it's ready for the new week, we can use B&B's poles, waders, and lures today.

I find myself whistling as I rummage through the shed to find the equipment we'll need. Even knowing I can't pursue anything with Taylor, I want to spend time with her. With Nick and Becca along as buffers, this fishing trip might be a great solution.

Unfolding a set of waders, Nick grins at me. "Someone's coming around to the idea of fishing today."

I flash him a mock glare. "I'm still not thrilled you didn't talk to me before making the plans, but yeah, I'm looking forward to it. I always have a good time fishing."

He raises his eyebrows questioningly. "And Taylor?"

I shrug, feigning nonchalance. "Fishing is more fun with *friends*."

Nick chuckles. "Uh-huh."

I press a tackle box into his chest. "Let's focus on getting the gear together." I pin him with a stern look. "Seriously, shut up about this today, please."

He mimes zipping his lips and drops the subject, just before Taylor and Becca peek their heads through the doorway.

Nick rubs his hands together. "Welcome, ladies! Let's get you outfitted."

Chapter Seventeen

Taylor

Whoever designed these waders did not have curvy women in mind. I struggle to pull them over my butt and hips, sliding them up an inch at a time. I would start hopping up and down if it weren't for my coworkers standing nearby putting on their own gear. It's embarrassing enough that I'm breaking a sweat while putting on pants over here.

Becca nudges me. "Do you need the next size up?" she asks quietly.

I harrumph. "No, then they'd be way too long."

The material finally gives way, and I almost fall over from the force. I steady myself, quickly glancing around to make sure no one is watching.

But of course, Jackson is. When I catch his eye, he quickly looks away, but not before I see the smirk on his lips. My face, already flushed from the effort of pulling these waders over my hips, heats even more.

Pointedly turning away from Jackson, I stretch the bib into place, fighting the waders again when I hoist it over my chest. I fasten the straps over my shoulders and then unfasten them. Yep. As I figured, the straps are way too loose. These waders are simultaneously too tight and too long. Clearly designed for a man. I huff as I adjust the clasp on the straps to shorten them.

When my waders are finally situated, I feel them compressing my butt and chest, pancaking two of my best features.

It's an inauspicious start to spending the day with my crush who friend zoned me three days ago, but I'm so excited to try fly-fishing that I don't even care.

After we have on the waders and shoes that look like hiking boots, we load into one of the ranch vans. It rattles as Nick drives us down the gravel driveway to the main road. The van feels empty with Nick and Jackson up front and Becca and me alone in the back.

A few minutes' drive down the main road, we pull into a campground and keep going on a dirt road with campsites on either side hosting tents, RVs, and camper vans. Nick pulls off and parks.

We tromp through the grass and shrubbery in our gear until the river comes into view. The bank is wide and rocky. When we get to the water's edge, Nick and Jackson keep walking into the river.

I stop to take in the view. Mountains rise in the distance, with steep hills angling up on the bank across from us. The green from the trees on the far side of the river reflects off the water, tinting it green as well. Near the bank, the water is calm and clear; I can see through to the rocky river floor. Out farther, an eddy churns the water as it rushes through.

"Come on!" Becca calls to me, and I step off the riverbank into the water. It's cold, but much like when we went white water rafting, the neoprene booties at the bottom of my waders and the wading boots over those blunt the chill. I can feel that the water's cold, but it makes my feet pleasantly cool instead of freezing cold.

I wade out to join the others. As I take a final step, Jackson pulls me back by my shoulders. "Careful," he warns. "The bed drops off here."

I peer through the ripples and see that, yes, I was about to step out onto nothing. The drop-off is steep.

Jackson hands me a fishing pole already set up with a lure and a bobber.

Back home, the fishing I've done is in the Gulf on family beach trips growing up. We used live shrimp as bait and fished from piers.

As Jackson demonstrates the process of casting and reeling, I realize that fly-fishing in a river is very different.

No live bait, for one. Instead, we'll use these artificial flies. And I can't believe how tiny the hooks are. Plus, we don't use bobbers at home. Instead, we hold a bit of the line in our hands and feel the bites in the tightening tension in the line.

Here, Jackson says that we have to watch the bobber carefully. If it looks like it's being pulled down even a little, we have to yank the rod up quickly to hook a nibbling fish. The nibble will be so subtle that holding the line won't help.

At least casting is mostly the same. As Nick helps Becca, Jackson directs me where to cast my line—in a spot right before the current picks up around the eddy. He says that I should cast there and then watch the bobber as the current takes the line farther downstream. Once it stops moving, I can reel it in and cast again.

He's about to give me a casting demonstration when I flip the spool release and flick the rod back and then forward again. The line makes that satisfying rhythmic whir sound, and the hook and bobber plop into the water before the current.

"Wow. Okay," Jackson sputters. "Great cast."

His praise warms me all the way through, and a content lightness fills my chest.

All too soon, though, I'm humbled again when Jackson yelps. "Watch the indicator! Pull up, pull up!"

I yank the pole straight up and start reeling in the line. It's empty.

"All right," Jackson says soothingly. "You almost had one there, but he got away. Try again."

Cast. Watch. Reel. Repeat.

I follow the pattern several more times. The bobber sinks, and I yank up on the pole, but the fish always get away.

I let out a frustrated growl as I reel in yet another empty line.

"You've got to yank the pole up really fast to set the hook," Jackson says. He gestures to my pole. "Here, want me to help?"

I nod and start to hand him the pole, but instead he tells me to cast. I do, and he moves up close behind me. He reaches his arms around me to hold the pole, and I'm enveloped in Jackson. My back is against his chest. His arms are caging mine on either side. His head is settled close, chin resting against my temple. He smells like soap and fresh mountain air.

Distracted by my very handsome fishing guide, I forget to watch the bobber.

Jackson must be watching, though, because suddenly, he's jerking the pole—and my arms—up. "Reel!" he huffs into my ear.

I turn the handle round and round and feel the resistance on the end of the line. Squealing, I keep spinning the handle until a huge fish pops above the surface.

Jackson—regrettably—lets me go, pulling a long-handled net out from behind his back, where it was tucked into his belt. He stomps through the water toward the fish and scoops it into the net.

"I caught a fish!" I shout.

Becca sloshes over and tackles me in a hug. "Woohoo!"

I laugh, happy to keep my footing during her attack.

As she steps back, Jackson swoops me up, wrapping both arms—including the arm holding the net—around my back and spinning me around.

"You did it!" he breathes into my ear.

I laugh and flush before he sets me down, and we examine the fish together.

"Rainbow trout," Nick announces from his vantage point a few feet away.

I look at Jackson. "Is it?"

"Yeah," he confirms. "A good-sized one, too."

He kneels to keep the trout in the water as he works the hook out of its mouth.

"Do you have your phone?" he asks. "Let's get a picture."

I hand my rod to Nick and my phone to Becca so I can kneel next to Jackson. A cool slosh of water travels up my thighs, but the waders keep my clothes and skin dry.

I hold the fish up with both hands evenly spaced in the center. It's about as long as my arm up to my sleeve.

Jackson quirks an eyebrow. "By yourself, or do you want me in the picture?"

Easy answer. "No, get in here!" I can't tug on his arm because my hands are full of fish, but he obeys, sliding closer.

We both beam at the camera as Becca takes a series of pictures.

"Should we bring him back to the ranch?" Nick teases.

Jackson, still kneeling close enough to me that my skin tingles with awareness, joins in. "Yeah, maybe we can get Chip to cook him for you."

My heart seizes at the thought of taking this guy from his watery home. "No, that's okay," I insist. "I don't like eating fish."

Nick bursts out laughing, and Jackson turns his face toward me, a playful grin on his lips. "You're from Florida, and you don't eat fish?"

I shrug. "To be fair, I'm not from *coastal* Florida. Ocala's in the interior."

Jackson shakes his head, smiling at me. "Let's release him, then."

He puts his hands over mine on top of the fish and guides my arms down into the water. Gently, we let him go, and he swims away.

"Be free, little fishy!" Jackson singsongs, and I can't help but admire how handsome he looks right now, boyish and carefree. Happy.

So different from the heaviness that burdened him by the creek the other night. His joy now is equally honest, but more rare.

A few minutes later, once my pole is reset and I'm back to casting, watching, and reeling, Jackson excuses himself and jogs off toward the campground's latrine.

Nick edges closer to me through the river. "Hey," he says in a low voice.

I look upstream at Becca, casting and reeling in her own little world. With furrowed brows, I turn to Nick. "Hi?"

"Jackson will be back soon, so I'll make this quick: it's worth it." His expression suggests I'm supposed to know what the heck he's talking about, but I don't.

I squint my eyes. "What?"

Nick sighs. "Getting to know Jackson. I know he's got all sorts of walls up, but they're worth breaking down. He's a great friend."

Nope, still confused. "Okay?"

"Jackson's really good at surface-level relationships. It's one of the reasons the guests love him so much. It's not my place to get into why, but when it comes to *meaningful* relationships, Jackson kind of sucks at them." Nick purses his lips. "Well, I guess it's more that he doesn't give them a fair chance. But anyway, he's worth getting to know."

He nods resolutely as if he's stamping the final word on a debate rebuttal.

"Good," I reply, meeting his gaze. "That's what I figured."

It's Nick's turn to look confused, but before he can say anything else, Jackson sloshes back into the river and over to us.

His eyes shift between Nick and me, a wrinkle on his forehead and a warning glare directed at Nick. "What's going on?"

Nick grins at him. "Nothing, buddy. Just helping Taylor with her indicator." He rubs his palms together. "Let's catch some more fish!"

Chapter Eighteen

Jackson

I'M OFF WORK AGAIN on Monday and head into town. I have a few errands to run, including letting my phone reconnect to data and sifting through the notifications.

As usual, it's mostly junk from social media or spammy emails. I have a few missed calls from my dad, though, so even though I'm sure I'll regret it, I call him back after I finish my errands.

"Where have you been?" he demands when he answers, and I'm already annoyed that I bothered to return his calls at all. I picture his brown eyes, the same as mine, narrowed in frustration.

"I don't have service at the ranch, remember? I'm in town today and saw that you called."

He makes a harrumph noise that tells me he either doesn't remember or doesn't care that I'm not in Boulder again this summer.

"Good thing. It's urgent."

My sigh rattles me down to my bones, and I run my hand across my eyes. "What's up?" I ask, already certain I know the answer.

"This is the one, Jack. This is the opportunity we've been waiting for."

I clench my teeth at the nickname.

"Uh-huh." I wait him out. He'll get to the point eventually and tell me how much money he wants me to "invest" with him.

"It's foolproof. A sure thing this time. The only problem is . . . I'm a little short on start-up cash."

He names a ridiculously large figure, and I choke back an indignant laugh.

"Dad, I don't have that kind of money."

"In the trust, you do."

The money in the trust my mother set up for me before she died was an inheritance she received from a great-aunt who she visited often as a child. When my parents divorced, the money was protected because of stipulations in Great-Aunt Bea's will. It's not a lot of money in the grand scheme of things, but it's enough for what Dad has planned now.

He's the trustee and as familiar with the parameters of the funds as I am. "You know I can't touch that money until I'm twenty-five." And even then, he won't see a dime of it.

He huffs. "Fine. I'll find another way, but you're missing out on a once-in-a-lifetime opportunity here."

The conversation, if you can call it that, wraps quickly after that. The same old, same old with my dad leaves me feeling unsettled. I shouldn't feel so disappointed anymore after one of his money grabs, but I guess it's something I may never be able to get used to. It's been hard for me to accept that he's not the man I used to think he was when I was a kid before my mom got sick.

In those days, we did everything together. I was his little buddy, a carbon copy of him in looks and energy. My mom said that we even laugh the same way.

Now that I'm an adult in my own right, I wonder if she'd still see similarities between me and my father. I hope not, but I worry that his example is baked into me. A destiny I can't escape.

Fortunately, the next part of my day includes climbing, which will help me put it all out of my mind.

I'm going to climb at the Island near Cody by the Buffalo Bill Dam. It's less than an hour from the ranch so it's been one of my go-to climbs over the last few summers.

This year, though, it's part of my official training plan. Gannett Peak is granite, so practicing on some of the oldest granite in Wyoming at the Island is good technical skills training. It's also predominantly vertical, like Gannett Peak will be, so it'll be good upper-body practice.

I'm also planning to try something new today. I'll wear a forty-pound pack as I climb, simulating what it might feel like to have that extra weight on me at Gannett Peak.

AFTER SPENDING FIVE HOURS treating the Island like my own personal circuit gym, tackling the various routes, I feel good. Tired, but not so exhausted that I worry about how I'll hold up on the big trip at the end of the summer.

And as expected, the phone call with my father this morning is a distant memory already.

By the time I pull into the staff parking lot at B&B in the early evening, I'm ready to eat, shower, and sleep, in that order. I've hit the tail end of dinner hour in the dining room, but I'm in no shape to mingle with the guests.

I've got on my black softshell mountaineering pants, but they're smeared with light gray granite dust, especially at my knees. My thighs are covered in white chalk dust from where I wiped my hands throughout the day. My sun hoodie is soaked in sweat to the point that I'm sure I reek.

Instead of tracking my funk through the lodge and dining room, I slip into the kitchen through the back door. Chip is packing up the leftovers from dinner.

"Can I make a plate to take to my cabin?" I ask him.

He looks me up and down and hands me a compostable to-go container. "Wash your hands before you touch anything."

I set the container on the counter and scrub my hands at the sink. Then I pile my plate high with meatloaf, mashed potatoes, green beans, and Chip's fresh homemade dinner rolls. I snag a fork and knife, promising Chip I'll return them in the morning as I head out the door to my cabin.

By the time I'm full and clean, I'm no longer tired. I sit with my legs spread-eagle on my bed, my bare back propped against a pillow on the headboard. Nick's not here; it's his night to help entertain the guests in the saloon.

I try reading a book, but I can't focus. The conversation with my dad this morning has come back to haunt me now that my mind isn't occupied by climbing anymore.

So, when Nick gets home, I'm not doing much of anything, and my guard is down.

When he sees me, Nick smiles predatorily. "Gotcha!"

I heave a sigh. "Got me what? What are you talking about?"

He sets his hands on his hips. "You've been avoiding me again. But now that we're both here, I have a question for you."

"Okay."

"I'm confused—"

I interrupt him with a smirk. "That's not too unusual for you, is it?"

Nick glares. "I'm *confused* because you told me Taylor isn't interested in you, but that's not what I saw when we went fishing the other day."

I groan. He's like a dog with a bone. "Nick."

"What's the problem, man? I mean, the chemistry is insane between the two of you, and—"

"Nick, let it go."

"I'm just saying. Seems like she'd be well worth it."

Obviously. Her worth has never been a question.

I give up and pull on a hoodie. "I'm going for a walk."

Opening the cabin door, I push out into the dusk. Nick—in a rare moment of wisdom—doesn't stop me.

I walk downhill past the lodge on the path that leads to the corral. The wide sky and the rhythm of putting one foot in front of the other are the perfect catalyst for processing my thoughts.

Fishing with Taylor the other day . . . I'm hard pressed to remember a more joyful time since before my mother passed away. Taylor's enthusiasm was infectious. She was so eager to learn, so excited when she caught a fish—not only that first time, but the two times after that as well.

I'm envious of her zeal for life and experiencing new things, even in the mundane. Some people might think that my risky hobbies fall into that same category—that I risk my life for fun because of the respect I have for my mortality, but I'm not sure that's true.

I'm starting to think that it's more about *avoiding* real life.

Stuffing my hands in the front pocket of my hoodie, I follow the path past the cabins without a conscious decision about where I'm going.

When I'm scaling a mountain, I need to be fully present simply to survive. I can't dwell on the day my mother found out about her cancer diagnosis when I was fifteen.

Flying a plane over gorgeous views keeps me from thinking about my dad's reaction to that diagnosis and how I spent my high school years taking care of my mom alone when the treatments left her weak and sick.

My hobbies definitely keep my mind off the years I've now spent living without her and the years yet to come that she'll miss. She'll never meet my future wife or children.

And if I don't think about these things, I don't have to deal with them. Pushing my body to the limit fills the hollowness inside me, even if only temporarily. The rush of adrenaline makes me feel alive when so many parts of me are still so numb.

Is there such a thing as self-medicating grief with risk taking? I don't know. Maybe I've got that.

Indoor climbing gyms were my refuge in those terrible years while Mom and I were fighting her cancer. When she first started treatments, I wasn't old enough to drive without a licensed adult in the car. So, I would drive her to the clinic after school one day every other week and then wait the several hours for her to finish so I could drive her home.

At first I waited with her, but I was a restless, scared kid, and I think my presence stressed my mom out. It was a godsend when we realized the building across the street from the infusion center was a rock climbing gym. My mom signed me up for an annual membership.

The tension in my shoulders ratchets up. There's some revelation here in these thoughts. Some self-awareness I can't quite grasp, like I have all the pieces but can't understand how they fit together.

In my line of work, everything is a trade-off. More thrust means a heavier engine, which affects lift. We need to find the exact point where all the competing physical forces meet an equilibrium.

My grief over my mother's death, my disillusionment with my father's decision to leave, my clinging to climbing as a coping mechanism, my aversion to relationships—they're all competing forces in my mind. But I'm not sure where they all meet or what that point of equilibrium means.

It's like I have all the data but can't see the pattern yet.

Without thinking about it, I turn around at the bridge before I get to the pole barn and walk back up the hill and past the lodge. My feet carry me on autopilot to my rock by the creek.

I sit and watch the sky turn orange and then purple until it finally deepens into a thick navy blue and reveals the sparkling stars.

Between the white noise of the creek water trickling past and the vastness of the night sky, my body relaxes, and I start to get sleepy again.

I'm in such a zen state that I don't hear the footsteps until they're almost on top of me. I snap my head up in time to see Taylor step into the clearing, the surprise on her face reflecting my own.

"Hi," I say stupidly.

She presses her hands to her cheeks, and her words come out in a rush. "I'm so sorry. I didn't know you would be here or else I wouldn't have come. It's just that I couldn't sleep, and this spot is so peaceful. I'm not stalking you or anything."

I huff a laugh. "I didn't think you were." I scoot to the side a safe distance and motion for her to join me on the rock. "I'm here for the same reason. Couldn't sleep."

She sits gingerly beside me, careful not to encroach on the space I've left between us. Meanwhile, everything in me is begging for her to squish on in, erase all the space between us. All the impediments making a relationship between us impossible.

At the same time, my scattered thoughts tonight prove she's better off if I keep my distance.

"I didn't realize this is your thinking spot."

I consider her words. "I don't know if I'd call it that, but I do like to come here at night to wind down."

We sit in companionable silence for several long moments. Her rigid posture slips enough that her hoodie-clad arm brushes against mine.

"You were off today, right?" Taylor asks.

"I was."

"What did you do?"

I shift, intentionally mashing our arms closer together. "I spent some time climbing at a place near Cody." I don't mention the phone call with my father.

Her eyes light up. "I've been dying to hear more about your rock climbing."

I laugh, but she's so earnest in her curiosity that I end up telling her about my day, and not only about the routes I climbed to help me prepare for Gannett Peak. She wants to know the technical terms for the gear I use and the other ways I've been training this summer.

"What do you think about while you're up there?" Taylor asks, a dreamy quality to her voice.

"My next step."

"That's it?"

"That's it. It's the difference between life or death. Climbing requires full concentration."

She yawns, sinking further into my side. "Sounds intense."

I check my watch and realize we've been out here talking for two hours. It's late, and Taylor has to get up early to take care of the horses tomorrow.

I nudge her shoulder with mine. "Come on. I'll walk you back to your cabin."

She yawns again, squeezing her eyes shut in the most adorable squint before sighing. She lays her head on my shoulder, and now I don't dare move.

"A few more minutes," she murmurs.

I wrap my arm around her shoulders and breathe in the smell of her floral shampoo as I rest my cheek against the top of her head. The weight of her against me soothes, warm and soft, and I find I'm not eager to leave either.

"A few more minutes," I agree.

Chapter Nineteen

Taylor

Without a discussion or verbal agreement, Jackson and I have started meeting at the rock by the creek almost every night once it gets dark outside.

Sometimes I get there first, and sometimes he does. Sometimes we talk. Sometimes we sit quietly and absorb the peace of the night. Sometimes we stay out there for hours, and sometimes it's a twenty-minute check-in.

Several weeks pass this way as June fades into July until it feels like we know everything about each other—favorite teachers from school, most embarrassing moments, most influential books, childhood best friends.

The only thing he won't talk about is his parents. If he mentions one or the other, he gets a sour look on his face and rushes ahead to his next point, refusing to linger.

There also seems to be a physical boundary he won't cross. He puts his arm around me, rubs circles on my back, and loves for me to rest my head on his shoulder, but when I try to intertwine our fingers, he pulls back.

When we make eye contact, electricity snaps between us. I drift toward him, and he leans toward me, but he doesn't close the gap. He swallows, blinks, and looks away.

I'm frustrated because I'm almost certain—my past embarrassing experiences won't let me be totally certain—Jackson's not only attracted to me, but he also feels this . . . this magnetism between us.

He obviously enjoys my company, so I'm not sure what the problem is. There's no way I'm going to broach the subject with him. Why? So I can be rejected with words instead of inaction? No, thank you.

But with every passing night together by the creek, I feel closer to him, more interwoven into his life. My feet are edging down Crush Trail on the way to falling over Love Cliff. And it's going to hurt when I go splat at the bottom of Heartbreak Canyon.

Tonight, after we each rehash our day, Jackson grins. "We're both off on Sunday."

"Okay?" From my spot leaning against his shoulder with his arm around me, my heart races. Maybe he'll ask me on a proper date.

He raises his eyebrows. "Our deal, remember? You hike with me if I ride a horse with you?"

Well, that's not a date. We agreed to this deal weeks ago.

I sit up, grinning anyway. "Trail ride on Sunday?"

He tightens his hold to pull my head back down to his shoulder. He clears his throat. "How about a hike?"

I'm second-guessing my earlier offer to rock climb with Jackson. I've never done it before, and it's dangerous. What if I fall?

"What do you have in mind?"

"The Dunraven Pass Trail up to Mount Washburn in Yellowstone. It's a hike, no rock climbing, but you'll get the benefit of the amazing view at the top. It's one of my favorite places in the park."

He says the last part with so much vulnerability in his voice that I recognize how nervous he is without seeing his face. Like this is a piece of himself he doesn't share casually. I don't have any information yet about how long the trail is or how steep, but it doesn't matter. I'm saying yes.

"Sounds beautiful," I say. "Of course I'm in."

I feel his relieved sigh on the top of my head as his breath tickles my scalp.

"It's a six-mile round-trip hike gradually up almost 1500 feet and then back down again, so it'll take us most of the day. I'll pack and carry everything we'll need; it'll be good training for my Gannett Peak trip."

I suck in air through my teeth. That sounds challenging, especially for someone not used to hiking on mountainous terrain or high elevation.

"We'll go completely at your pace," Jackson reassures me, as if reading my mind. "We can take as long as you need."

I nod, and he goes on and on about what I should wear and bring and everything we'll see. His excitement is endearing, and I press the side of my head more tightly against him. I doze off to the sound of his voice.

Sunday morning starts off foggy and cool. As Jackson recommended, I dress in layers: sneakers and thick yoga pants, a tank top under a T-shirt, and a fleece jacket. Even though it's July, the temperature won't get much higher than seventy degrees, especially the higher up we go. I pull my hair into a ponytail and slather my face and neck in sunscreen.

When I step onto the front porch of my cabin, Jackson's already waiting for me, sitting in one of the wooden chairs with a large hiking pack next to him. He jumps up when he sees me, his smile stretching across his whole face.

"Ready?" he asks.

I prop my hands on my hips. "Don't I look ready?"

Jackson takes his time perusing me from head to toe. He takes a step closer and lifts his hand toward my face. My heart stutters as his thumb caresses my cheek.

"You've got a bit of sunscreen that didn't rub all the way in," he says, though he sounds as breathless as I feel. "But yeah, you look ready." He studies my face a moment longer. "And beautiful."

"Oh, good," I joke to ease the tension. "I'm trying to impress the bighorn sheep."

He chuckles. "Mission accomplished, then."

When we turn to walk toward the staff parking lot, Jackson puts his hand on the small of my back to guide me along. It's a good thing, too, because I would have gone straight for one of the ranch vans.

Jackson gestures to a black truck parked on the far end. "We're taking my truck. I have an annual pass to get into the park."

I'm not sure I even realized that Jackson has a vehicle here, though of course it makes sense. Boulder isn't nearly as far away as Ocala, and with all his training sessions, he'd want his own transportation.

He opens the passenger door for me, and I step on the running board to climb in. The interior is nice—black leather seats and a massive screen on the front dash with enough buttons around it to program a satellite. Jackson is an aeronautical engineer, so maybe he *could* actually program a satellite from his truck.

Do aeronautical engineers program satellites?

Jackson stows his pack in the back of the truck and joins me in the cab. He pushes a button on the dash labeled "Start," and the engine roars to life.

"Your truck is really nice," I tell him. "I'm used to old work trucks that sputter before the engine decides to turn over."

He chuckles. "Thanks." He leans closer and points at some buttons near me. "Those control the seat warmers if you want."

Ooh, seat warmers! I turn the dial until I start to feel heat on my lower back and thighs.

"It feels great on my muscles after a grueling climb," Jackson explains.

His words invite me to rove my eyes over those muscles, visible underneath the tight-fitting jacket on his arms. The fabric of his gray pants—they look like a cross between cargo pants and fishing pants—is stretched over his thigh muscles, which are toned and defined, but not bulky.

Jackson's busy backing out of the parking spot and focusing on the foggy road, so he doesn't notice my wandering eyes as they take in the backward baseball hat that cuts across his forehead.

"It'll take us about an hour and a half to get to the trailhead." He turns to me and winks before pulling out of the B&B driveway onto the main road. "So, you might want to give your eyes a rest while we drive."

I blush. *Okay, maybe he did notice.*

I turn my face to the front and pretend it's the seat warmers making my cheeks overheat.

"I got us some breakfast," he continues. He jerks a thumb behind him. "That bag in the back seat. Chip helped me pack a few things last night. Breakfast burritos."

I reach into the backseat and return with a brown paper bag containing two burritos wrapped in aluminum foil.

"You want yours?" I ask.

Jackson sticks out his hand in assent. Before I give it over, I peel back the foil around the top to expose the tortilla underneath. The savory smell wafts toward me, and the breath I inhale makes my mouth water.

I hand Jackson his food and start unwrapping mine.

"What's in it?"

Through a mouthful of burrito, Jackson's voice is garbled. "Whole wheat tortilla, scrambled eggs, avocado, and cubed sweet potatoes."

I take a bite and moan appreciatively. "Oh, yum."

Jackson darts his eyes over to me and swallows. His lips quirk up in a grin. "Remind me to bring you food more often."

I hum. "Yes, please."

When we get to the park entrance, Jackson shows the digital pass on his phone to the woman at the gate, along with his ID. She scans his phone screen and waves us forward.

I notice familiar sights as we drive toward the trailhead. After a while, Jackson slows the truck and points out my window.

"Check it out. A grizzly."

I gasp as I spot the huge bear rambling through the trees next to the road. He's on all fours, his thick fur such a dark brown that it appears almost black in the morning light. If I didn't know he was there, I would have had trouble seeing him among the cover of the trees.

"How did you even see that?"

Jackson grins. "Years of practice."

We continue on, past the Yellowstone General Stores in the area near Fishing Bridge, the parking lot already crowded with cars and trucks.

When we come to a fork in the road, Jackson turns right, the opposite way we went when we were here with the group of guests last month.

"We'll be passing through Hayden Valley soon," he tells me. "There are usually herds of bison there this time of year. Sometimes they even cause traffic jams as they cross the road."

I watch out my window, and sure enough, soon I see dozens of bison in the grassy plains around us.

"It never gets old," I marvel, keeping my attention on the herds.

"For me, either," Jackson admits. "Even though I saw them out here a few days ago on the guest tour. July is their mating season, so they congregate a lot more."

"This place is so beautiful," I say with a sigh.

He grins. "Wait until you see the view from Mount Washburn."

Chapter Twenty

Jackson

The fog has largely burned off by the time we get to the trailhead. There's a small parking lot and a public latrine, with several groups of people milling around on the sidewalk as they prepare for their hikes.

I pull into one of the empty parking spots and turn off the truck. I unbuckle and face Taylor.

"I'll carry everything we need in the pack—snacks, extra water, emergency equipment—but it should only take us a couple of hours to get to the top. We'll go at your pace, like I said, and we're not in a rush, so take your time if you need to."

Taylor's expression takes on a nervous glint. Being from Florida, I can only assume that she's not used to elevation when she hikes. She's been in Wyoming long enough that her body should have fully acclimated to the lower oxygen levels in the air here by now, which should keep her from huffing and puffing too much as we walk.

"When we get to the top, we can have lunch and take pictures and rest for a while," I continue. "There's a restroom up there, too."

She looks relieved. "So, I'm not going to need to do any off-roading after I drink all that water?"

I laugh. "No, you should be good." I glance at the latrine near the far end of the parking lot. "Let's both go before we set out, though, okay?"

She grins. "Sounds like a plan."

We take care of business and approach the trail at the same time as a middle-aged couple in matching track suits.

As much as I'd love to be alone with Taylor as we hike, having at least three people is the standard recommendation because it deters bears from approaching.

The hike up to the peak is peaceful, slow, and steady. The rigor of the rocky trail is way below my skill level, though the rocks I added to my pack to weigh it down make this hike good training for my big trip next month.

Taylor keeps pace, and though I can tell the uphill climb is challenging her, she seems to be enjoying herself.

It's a gorgeous day to be outside. After the fog burns off, the sky turns a bright, clear blue. The air is cool, especially as we get higher up the mountain, but it's pleasant against my face that's flushed with physical exertion.

When we reach the top, Taylor marvels at the bird's-eye view—the dramatic cliffs of the Grand Canyon of the Yellowstone, the flat grasses of Hayden Valley, the vast blue of Yellowstone Lake in the distance. I've seen it all before.

I'm watching *her*.

How the light catches in her eyes, illuminating flecks of hazel hiding in the brown. How the wind blows strands of her hair out of the ponytail, how they whip across her face and stick to her lips. How the curve of her hips makes the perfect perch for her hands as she takes it all in.

Taylor pulls her phone from a pocket on the side of her leggings and snaps a string of what must be nearly identical pictures. She turns and waves me over, holding her phone above her head and smiling so brightly that I'm momentarily blinded.

I jog to her, and she reaches for me, her hand sliding over my biceps. "Can you take a photo for me?" she asks.

I take the outstretched phone, and she poses. When she's done, she comes toward me again, and I hold out the phone for her to take. She bypasses her phone and lays her hand on my forearm.

"Take one with me," she urges.

As if in a daze, I drop my pack on the ground and walk with Taylor back near the edge. Switching the phone camera to selfie mode, I hold it at arm's length.

Taylor smooshes her cheek next to mine within the frame, and I'm distracted by the smooth chill of her skin against my stubble.

I take a picture, and it's us, but without much of the scenic background.

"Want me to take one for you?" calls Darlene, the female half of the couple we hiked up with.

"Yes, please!" Taylor passes over her phone, and I snake my arm around her waist. She rests her hand against my back as we smile for the picture.

It feels . . . natural, necessary. Comfortable to hold her like this. At the same time, my body buzzes toward the warmth of her hand on my back and her hip and shoulder against mine. Like that first cup of coffee in the morning—how it's an easy and expected part of my daily routine but still satisfying with every sip. Warm, cozy, and energizing.

"You are such a cute couple!" Darlene croons as she hands Taylor's phone back to her.

"Oh, no, we're not . . . he's not . . ." Taylor blushes as she rushes to explain.

I stop her with a squeeze to her waist where I'm still holding her. "Thank you."

Taylor gives me a confused look. Letting go of her, I reach for her phone. "Let's get a few more of you from this angle," I suggest.

She blinks and shakes her head, moving where I'm directing her.

After Taylor gets her fill of pictures, I lead her to the indoor observation deck in the fire lookout tower.

"Ready for lunch?" I ask her.

She nods, and I scope out the room for someplace to sit. It's a busy day on the mountain, so all the benches are taken. I find a spot on the floor and unload the food from my pack.

I pass Taylor an apple, a baggie of peanut butter, and a stick of beef jerky before digging into my own serving.

"Is it weird that I'm actually not very hungry?" Taylor asks after she swallows a bite of apple mixed with peanut butter.

"Nah. The higher elevation slows digestion. Eat as much as you can comfortably stomach, though, because you'll need the energy for the hike back down." I pass her a full bottle of water from my pack. "And drink lots of water."

We fall into conversation as we eat—about our energy levels after the hike up, the view, how windy it is at the peak.

"I've never lived near mountains or even hills, so an experience like this is so cool for me. I could tell you some things about swamps, though," Taylor jokes.

I swallow a bite of my beef jerky. "Growing up in Colorado, there were mountains on every horizon for me. My mom always said that views of mountains and oceans are proof that God loves us."

The words are out before I realize I've introduced my mother into the conversation.

I glance at Taylor. The look on her face tells me that she expects me to brush past it again, like I do every time I accidentally mention either of my parents. I nearly do. Instead, I take a deep breath and, ignoring everyone else in the room, stare out the window at the bright sky behind Taylor, telling her about my mom.

"She was . . . extraordinary. She could turn the most mundane day into magic. She loved flowers and seashells and horses. She was an elementary school teacher. Second grade."

I hazard a glance at Taylor. She's sitting perfectly still, her eyes, wide and soft, trained on me. She leans forward. I take another breath and continue.

"When I was fifteen, she was diagnosed with breast cancer." Taylor gasps quietly, and I drop my eyes back to the ground. "My dad . . . his first reaction was to divorce her. Said he wasn't cut out to be a caretaker."

That day is as clear in my memories as if it had been last week. My dad's heavy suitcases sitting by the front door. My mom with red eyes, trying to hold strong for me. His callous, whispered invitation for me to go with him. My moment of shame when I considered it, even for a second.

I was fifteen, and while Mom had always been the comforting parent, Dad had always been the fun parent. So, for a second, I considered how easy it would be to live with him, away from the nightmare of my mother's sickness. I still haven't forgiven myself for that, for being even a little bit like him.

"I spent most of my high school years with her at outpatient centers while she got treatments. I'd drive her there and wait around while the doctors ran tests.

"There was an indoor rock climbing gym across the street. It wasn't something I'd ever been interested in, but I needed somewhere to blow off steam, and it was close enough that I felt like I could rush back if Mom needed me.

"She tried not to need me. She tried really hard. She wanted me to be a typical teen and not have to spend my free time in hospitals and clinics. But I was all she had, and as much as she didn't want to rely on me, she couldn't do it alone.

"She died when I was eighteen," I finish quietly. "A few months before my high school graduation."

I look at Taylor again, and her eyes are shining.

"And by then, you were hooked on rock climbing," she guesses, and I appreciate that's the piece of the story she chooses to focus on.

More than hooked, though. I *needed* the rock climbing. Needed a way to forget my dad's cowardice, my mom's suffering. Forget the bright, sunny spring day of her funeral, the hollow ache in my chest.

"Pretty much," I mumble, rubbing the heels of my hands into my eyes.

Taylor rises to her knees and, without warning, climbs into my lap, both legs off to one side and her head in the crook of my neck. She wraps her arms around me and squeezes.

Something inside me shudders and settles, like a building easing onto its foundation. I only hesitate a moment before I fold my arms around her and return the embrace.

I nuzzle my face into her hair. It smells like the mountains and flowers and sweat. I close my eyes and release a long breath that leaves my body sagging around hers.

Her fleece jacket is fuzzy underneath the palms of my hands, curved to hold onto her sides. Her breath, warm and wet, tickles the skin on my neck. Her hands clutch near the top of my spine, fingers splaying into my hair and tangling there.

I forget that we're sitting on the floor in a crowded observation room. Forget that we're supposed to just be friends. Forget that I can't have her forever.

A loud laugh echoes from the other side of the room, and everything rushes back into my consciousness.

I pull my head back and drop my arms. Taylor unwinds herself from around my neck, her cheeks pink as she scoots off my lap and back into her own space.

"I'm glad you told me," she says quietly. "Glad you're trusting me."

"I do trust you," I murmur.

Another bashful look in her direction, and I clear my throat. "We should get going, though. We'll want to be down before any afternoon storms roll in."

The forecast is clear, but I need to escape this little room where I bared my secrets to the woman I'm finding it harder and harder to hide from. I need to get back to the wide open skies.

We finish eating, and I gather our trash and deposit it into one of the receptacles in the room. We each use the restroom before we make our way outside.

Walking the trail heading back down the mountain has its own set of challenges. Gravity and momentum are on our side, but each step will put an uncomfortable weight on our knee joints as we descend.

I stop to tighten the laces on my hiking boots, and Taylor follows suit with her sneakers.

"Oh wait! I almost forgot." I rummage in the side pocket of my pack for the small baggie I put there earlier. "I have a treat for us before we start hiking."

I open the bag and angle it toward Taylor.

"Gummy bears?" she asks, a grin lifting the corners of her lips.

"It's strategic," I defend. "The quick hit of sugar will give us an energy boost." I reach into the bag with my free hand and grab a few pieces of candy, popping them into my mouth. "Besides, they're delicious."

Taylor giggles and helps herself to a handful, and I put the baggie back in my pack.

We've only gone a few yards down the trail when Taylor slips on a patch of scree, her foot flying out in front of her. She gasps, but my hands are on her arms in seconds, keeping her upright.

"Watch out."

"Yeah," she says in a shaky voice. "Thanks."

I let go of her arm, trailing my hand down to hers. Heart pounding, I tease my fingers against hers, brushing them in a way I can probably play off as unintentional if I need to.

Taylor blushes again, and looking me in the eye, knits our fingers together, her palm gliding against mine.

Returning her gaze, I can't help the grin that overtakes my face. I shrug. "Safety first."

She laughs and tugs on my hand, urging me down the trail.

Chapter Twenty-One

Taylor

Holding Jackson Hollis's hand for an hour and a half as we hike down Mount Washburn was not on my bingo card for today. But I'm not mad about it.

We're both quiet on the drive back to the ranch. It's been an amazing day—a perfect day—but tiring, too. From the strain and exhaustion of the hike itself to the emotional weight of Jackson finally sharing about his parents, I'm pleasantly mushy, my brain and muscles hazy against the heated seat of Jackson's truck.

We're back at the ranch by three, passing under the B&B arch behind two cars of arriving guests. Fortunately, the staff parking lot takes us around to the backside of the lodge, so we escape any need to greet the guests or play host if we come across them.

"What are you up to for the rest of the afternoon?" I ask Jackson after he races around the truck to open the passenger door for me.

He shrugs. "Nothing."

He puts his hand out to help me down, and my fingers burn with memory as they brush against his calloused skin.

"I was going to sit on my cabin's front porch and draw, if you'd like to grab a book or something and join me."

His lips curl up in a lazy smile. "Yeah. I'll meet you there."

I take the short walk to my cabin, my muscles protesting every step of the way, and push open the door. Becca's down at the lodge greeting guests, but I know later tonight she'll pump me for details about my day.

Pulling off my sneakers and socks, I wiggle my toes and groan. Even my toenails are sore. How is that possible?

I don't bother changing my clothes, but I wash my face in the bathroom before gathering my sketch pad and pencils to set up on the porch.

My artistic process is one I've honed over the years, and it works for me. I usually paint or draw from a photograph, my phone propped in front of me, the screen set to stay awake. I don't recreate the picture exactly, though. I add in detail and colors, my own bits of flair.

I'm deep into sketching one of the B&B horses, Cleo, when Jackson approaches. I see the containers of food in his arms, and my stomach grumbles, suddenly starving.

"Oh, you saint of a man! What did you bring?" I tease.

He chuckles, setting the food down on the little table between the two chairs on the porch. He holds up his hand and starts ticking off the list on his fingers. "Blueberry lemon muffins, carrot sticks, yogurt with homemade granola, and some of Chip's peanut butter cookies, fresh from the oven."

I already have the container open and a bite of muffin in my mouth before he finishes the list.

I drop my head back against the chair and close my eyes. "So good!" I moan.

The heat of Jackson's gaze lingers on me as I take another bite. "I figured you'd be hungry after hiking all day. I know I am."

He flops into the chair next to me and breaks another of the food containers open. He scoops up two carrot sticks, dips them into a blob of yogurt, and crunches into them.

I wrinkle my nose. "Did you eat a carrot covered in yogurt?"

He swallows the bite and nods. "Yeah, it's good. Why?"

"I've never heard of that combination." I say, polishing off my muffin and reaching for another.

Jackson shrugs. "It's pretty much the same thing as vegetable dip, except I didn't add any seasonings."

I tilt my head to inspect his plate. "It's *plain* yogurt?"

His ears turn red when he answers. "Vanilla flavored."

A rumble of laughter moves up through my chest until I stifle it in my throat. But it's no use. A giggle slips through and soon I'm doubled over, tears in my eyes.

Once the peals mute to chuckles, I wipe my eyes and regard Jackson. He's got a bit of a grumpy thing going on with his face, but I read the amusement mixed with mild embarrassment in his eyes.

"I'm sorry," I gasp out. "You're just so . . . you're so . . ." I can't finish my thought, not because I don't know what comes next, but because I'm not sure I want to share it. I bring my hand in front of my mouth to keep it in.

"So *what*?" Jackson challenges, his gaze darkening.

I shrug and grin at him behind my hand.

He reaches forward and circles his fingers around my wrist, pulling my hand down to my lap.

"So *what*?" he repeats, eyes locked on mine.

"Adorable," I whisper, and I hope he understands that I mean that as a compliment.

I doubt grown men like being called adorable, like a kitten or fluffy duckling, but that's not exactly what I mean. I mean that the brightness of his smile, the crinkle in the corner of his eyes, the way he moves and risks and cares—everything about him—is precious to me. I mean that I want to know all his weird food preferences, all his thoughts and his scars. I mean that I want nothing more than to adore him for as long as he'll let me.

Even though I don't explain it out loud, I think he gets it, because his eyes soften into pools of melted chocolate, his long lashes fluttering up and down as he blinks at my choice of adjective.

"Adorable, huh?" His voice is gravel churning barely above a whisper. "And what does that make you?"

Yours, I want to say.

"You tell me."

His gaze turns molten. His fingers are still wrapped around my wrist, his thumb brushing across my skin in firm, rhythmic circles.

The same thrum of tension I've felt with him before—at Artist Point, at our spot by the creek—thickens the air between us, and I know he wants to kiss me.

I want him to . . . badly. More than I've ever wanted anything else before in my life.

I tilt forward, so tuned in to Jackson and the way his body is fizzing that I notice when he echoes the motion, tipping himself toward me ever so slightly.

I close my eyes in an extended blink and swallow, sitting in the buzz of the moment.

Jackson clears his throat, and then his hand is gone from my wrist. I open my eyes in time to see him lean back in his chair, far away from me and with a shell-shocked expression.

Hot disappointment burns into my lungs like a breath of sticky Ocala air in August.

He clears his throat again. "I'll have to think on it," he says, and I'm confused about what he means until I realize he's responding to my earlier challenge. He'll have to think to come up with an adjective for me, he's saying.

I don't know what happened to our perfect kiss moment, but I'll wait with bated breath to find out how he wants to describe me.

Chapter Twenty-Two

Jackson

Now that Taylor has fulfilled her part of our deal—not only climbing a mountain with me but crushing it in the process—I know it's time for me to pay up.

Logically, I understand that I shouldn't be so afraid of horses. Now that I'm an adult, they don't look nearly as giant as they did when I was eight. The horse throwing me then was a fluke caused by my inexperience, and it's not likely to happen again.

I'm really not looking forward to riding, though.

And yet, I'm already planning my trail ride with Taylor, figuring out when we're both off work again, imagining how beautiful she'll look with her eyes bright and happy, doing one of her favorite things in the world.

Turns out I'll do most anything—including facing my greatest fear—if it means spending more time with Taylor.

Spending time with her, though, is a minefield of temptation. My self-control was stretched to its limit on our hike, and afterward, sitting on her porch.

She said I'm *adorable*, and I can't think of anything cuter or more tragic than gorgeous Taylor Steed-Gallagher finding *me*, a commitment-phobic daredevil, adorable. She deserves better than my fleeting attention; she deserves someone who can offer her forever, and a perfect, golden ratio of a first kiss she'll want to remember for the rest of her life.

I can't stand the thought of her later regretting that she let me take that kiss.

THE FOLLOWING WEEK, DENNIS lets the activity guides know that we have a smaller than normal group of guests signed up for the Yellowstone tour. Apparently, many of them have been to the park before and would rather spend their time at B&B riding horses. Leanne has to adjust the wranglers' schedules so that they're all available Wednesday to lead trail rides. They're planning a "kids' ride" for the small group of children hanging out at the ranch that day.

The change in plans gives me an idea. I talk to Dennis to make sure Nick and Danny can handle the Yellowstone trip without me. Then, I see if Leanne can help me arrange a surprise for Taylor.

On Wednesday morning, I show up at the stables in my boots and cowboy hat. Other than when I'm on duty welcoming guests to the ranch on Sundays, they don't get a lot of use, but a trail ride is the ideal occasion.

Besides, I've seen the way Taylor ogles me in this getup on the Sundays we work together. She must like the cowboy look, even though in actuality I'm the furthest thing from a cowboy.

My cowboy attire is part of her surprise.

I wait out of sight while Taylor and Leanne get six kids situated on their horses.

Taylor's so good with the kids. I watch her help a little girl onto a horse and then stop and listen while the girl, whose face looks very serious, says something to her that I can't hear. Taylor pats the little girl's leg and nods, answering the concern with reassuring words.

A little boy already in his saddle calls out, "Miss Taylor, did you see my boots?"

Taylor makes a show of admiring his black-and-red boots, acting like she's going to pull them off his feet to steal them for herself. "I bet these would fit me!" she teases. The boy giggles like crazy.

One night sitting on our rock by the creek, Taylor told me how much she wants to be a mother someday, although hearing the wistfulness in her voice as she talked, it sounded like her version of "someday" is much sooner than mine.

I want kids someday, too, but it's not something I can imagine clearly. Thoughts of a wife and family are murky in my head, something I'd like to have, but so far in the future that they're hardly worth mentioning now.

It's obvious Taylor will be a wonderful parent. Me, on the other hand . . . well, considering the example I had of fatherhood—and my risky hobbies—I'm wary of my potential.

It's another reason this attraction between Taylor and me can't go beyond harmless flirtation. She's looking for someone that I'm not.

"Hold on," I hear Taylor say when all the kids are ready to go. "Why is Horace saddled up? No one's riding him this week."

I take that as my cue to strut into the corral, my thumbs hooked into the front pockets of my jeans.

"I think somebody is," Leanne says to Taylor, nodding her head toward me. She winks before she moves to the other end of the corral to mount her horse and get the kids lined up for the ride.

"Jackson?" Taylor glances around as if looking for an explanation.

I walk closer, keeping a nervous eye on the two horses standing behind her. "You climb a mountain with me, I take a trail ride with you, right? That was our agreement."

Despite my nerves, I can't help but smile when understanding dawns across her face and leaves her beaming.

"But you're at Yellowstone on Wednesdays."

I lift my hands and shrug. "They didn't need me today."

She claps her hands twice. "Oh my goodness, what a fun surprise!" Her hands are clasped together in front of her chest. "This will be so fun!"

With three steps and a bounce, she wraps her arms around my neck and hugs me. Instinctively, my hands go to her waist, then stretch around to her back as I return the embrace. My heart races with her warm body in my arms. She fits perfectly, and I'm not ready to let go. Maybe ever. I lift her up and spin around once, her laugh a joyful song in my ear.

Forget the horses, because now my anxiety is stemming from my reaction to Taylor's happiness. One thought hits me between the eyes and leaves me stunned: this is more than flirtation. My feelings are centered on much more. I want her glee. I want her enthusiasm. I want her zeal for life; a zest that doesn't come from cheating death like the fleeting high

I feel from my hobbies, but that radiates from her daily as she cherishes the tiniest delights.

The more time I spend with her, the more I'm noticing the smallest, most beautiful details of the land and mountains I already love. And the more I'm memorizing the tiniest details of her face, down to the freckles on her cheeks and the individual sparkles in her eyes.

I really don't know what to do with any of that.

When I finally set her on her feet again, she slides her hands past my shoulders until they're resting on my upper arms. She turns her face toward mine, her whole being glowing like the sun.

Taylor gestures to a white-and-brown horse behind her who looks huge but stands calmly as if waiting for us to finish our conversation. "Like I promised, Horace is a sweetie pie."

She squeezes my arms twice in reassurance. "You'll be safe," she says, low enough that only I can hear her. "You ready?"

I grimace. "As much as I can be."

Taylor giggles and leads me toward Horace. She explains how to get in the saddle, and with one hand in the horse's mane—she insists that it won't hurt him, but I'm worried he's cataloging this abuse for later retribution—I fit my foot into the stirrup and push myself up, swinging my other leg over the saddle.

And I'm sitting on a horse.

Taylor hands me the reins and tells me how they're the steering wheel, brakes, and gas pedal all in one. She adjusts my stirrups until they're at a comfortable height for my feet.

"Horace is trained and has done this trail dozens of times. He'll follow the horse in front of him, so you won't really need to direct him much." She nods toward where Leanne and the kids are lined up waiting for us. "We'll be at the back of the line. I'll stay right behind you."

I look down at the top of her head. "Reckless," I say.

She squints up at me. "Huh?"

The edges of my mouth start to form a smile, but Horace takes a step forward and I grimace instead, clutching the reins.

"A word for you," I explain through clenched teeth. "I told you the other day I'd have to think on it. Now I'm going with 'reckless' because you get up on these giants every day for *fun*."

She laughs. "That's funny coming from you, mister rock climbing pilot." She purses her lips. "I don't like it. Keep thinking."

This time I do smile. "Yes, ma'am."

With one last grin in my direction, she hops on her horse, and we join the group.

Leanne leads us slowly out of the corral, over the bridge, and down the road toward B&B's front entrance. I start getting anxious that we're going to go onto the main street and the cars will scare the horses.

I want to turn around and see Taylor, but I'm worried even that small movement will disturb Horace, or he'll think I'm giving him some sort of command that I don't understand.

I feel her presence behind me, though, like my back is turned toward a stove holding a pot of warm milk waiting to be mixed with pieces of dark chocolate for hot cocoa.

"You're doing great, Jackson." Her voice is even and bright, and I risk a glance over my shoulder to see her smile.

The brown horse Taylor's riding stops and steps back, and she urges it forward again with soft words and a kick of her heels.

I swallow. "Your horse seems more . . . twitchy than mine."

Taylor laughs. "Pistol can be a little ornery, but she's nothing I can't handle." And she winks.

See? Reckless.

Ahead of me, Leanne leads our line of horses off the B&B driveway into the grass. I notice a thin, well-worn trail of dirt stretching into the distance. It doesn't look wide enough for a human hiker, so I'm amazed when Horace takes step after step without his hooves touching the grass on the edges of the trail.

Leanne is saying something up ahead. I strain my ears to hear her, afraid it's some sort of warning or other life-and-death information I'm missing.

"She's telling the kids about the plants and flowers," Taylor says. "Relax. Look around. All you need to do is enjoy the ride."

Chapter Twenty-Three

Taylor

JACKSON WAS NOT KIDDING when he said he's afraid of horses. He's fidgety sitting there on Horace, his head moving to watch the feet of the horse in front of him and then toward the front of the line as if he's expecting a disaster around every bend of the trail.

Horace is the perfect horse for him, though, because Horace doesn't care how badly the human connected to him is freaking out. He does not spook easily.

I hate how anxious Jackson obviously is, but I love that he's here on a trail ride with me . . . and my boss and six children. It's not a romantic ride by any means, except for the fact of what Jackson is putting himself through to make me happy.

And I am.

Especially with the way he looks dressed in jeans, boots, and a Stetson. Not surprisingly, I've always had a thing for cowboys. Not that Jackson is a cowboy—I giggle at the thought—but seeing him dressed as one and on a horse, combined with everything else I know about his loyalty and kindness, it's hard to remember that I'm not supposed to fall in love with him.

We plod along in our line. The trail we picked for today runs along Libby Creek, stretching north from the ranch into the foothills of Sleeping Giant Mountain. It's one of our shorter, easier trails, and generally one we take kids on for their first ride, or, in cases like this, when we have more children than adults in the group.

This is the same trail I first rode when the horses arrived at B&B. It was only two months ago, but it feels like a lifetime. By now, I know this trail like the back of my hand, and the horses do, too.

It's new for Jackson, though. The further we go, the more he trusts Horace's calm, and he starts looking around at the trees and mountains that surround us.

I feel a thrill of satisfaction at being able to show Jackson something for once. He's an expert on this area, but he doesn't know the horse trails like I do.

Ahead of us, Leanne tells the kids stories about the area. None of us know if they're true or not, but they're local legends that are fun to pass along.

"One summer," Leanne begins, and I know she's warming up to tell my favorite ranch ghost story, "one of the B&B Ranch activity guides went for a hike. While he was hiking, he found a small rubber boa snake that was injured. It had a cut on its side.

"He brought the snake with him back to the ranch and kept it in a plastic container in his cabin. Everyone said he should set it free, but he was convinced the snake wouldn't survive in the wild until it healed.

"But then one night, the guide and his cabinmate woke up to a terrible commotion in their cabin! The snake's bin was knocked over, the lid off, and the snake was gone. They spent the rest of the night and most of the morning searching for it everywhere in the cabin, but they couldn't find it.

"Legend has it that the ghost of the little rubber boa still haunts cabin fifteen to this day."

Our line of horses is curving around a bend in the trail, so I have a good vantage point to see the children's faces in profile across the field of grass and wildflowers. The older ones are laughing, while some of the younger kids are wide-eyed at the tale.

In front of me, Jackson scoffs.

Giddy that he's reacting to something other than his anxiety, I call out, "What?"

Carefully and slowly, Jackson turns at the waist until he can see me. "That story." He shakes his head. "I was here the summer that supposedly happened. It was my first summer at B&B. The hiker was my cabinmate. We were hiking together when he somehow caught a snake. It wasn't injured; he was just kind of a jerk who didn't follow the rules about leaving wildlife alone. He wanted it as a pet and wouldn't listen to a word I said about it.

"After he fell asleep that first night, I took the snake outside and set it free. There was no mysterious commotion, and that snake is probably still alive today in its natural habitat."

He shakes his head again, lips quirking up in the corners. "Ghost snake. Please."

While I knew that the story had to be either partially or entirely made up, hearing Jackson lay out the truth so plainly is a bit of a letdown.

I scrunch my nose. "Well, that's no fun."

He faces forward again and shrugs. "Taking animals out of the wild and putting them into captivity is what's no fun."

I giggle, and he turns to look at me again, a grin forming on his face. "What?"

"You," I answer with another round of giggles. "So serious."

His grin shifts into a dazzling smile. With all the ease of someone who could ride horses before she could walk, I slide my phone out of my saddle bag. Before he can turn around or drop his smile, I snap a picture.

"Hey!" he protests. "What was that for?"

"Posterity," I quip, examining the photo on my screen. The lighting is gorgeous, Jackson's handsome face shining under his Stetson, and his eyes soft. The mountains rise up behind him, the blue of the sky punctuated with soft white clouds.

My voice comes out dreamy, on a sigh. "Perfect."

"Are you going to paint me?" he teases.

"I only paint horses," I retort.

Usually, that's true. I don't paint people. I'm mostly inspired by horses and the beauty of landscapes in nature.

I glance at the photo again. I might paint this, though. Him. When the next few weeks are over and I'm back home with only my memories of Jackson to keep me company, I might paint this portrait as a way of keeping him with me. It's a painful, lonely thought.

I lift my gaze from the photo back to the man himself, or the back view of him anyway, because he's turned around to face the front. He looks comfortable on the horse now, unafraid and strong. Torturously handsome.

Wordlessly, I tuck my phone back into the saddlebag. A headache forms behind my eyes as I realize that it's already too late. I'm pretty sure I've fallen completely in love with Jackson Hollis.

BACK AT THE STABLES after the trail ride, Leanne and I help the kids dismount and release them to their waiting parents.

We start the process of untacking and grooming the horses. Jackson loiters, trying to help, but after two hesitant attempts, it's clear he's going to slow us down more than anything. I send him away with a hug and a smile, promising to see him in the lodge for lunch when I finish here.

I'm quieter than normal as we work—still absorbing the realization I had during the ride about my feelings for Jackson—but if Leanne notices, she doesn't comment on it.

I feel her watching me, though.

Leanne is my boss this summer, but we've become friends, too. She's ten years older than me, so it's maybe more of a mentor-mentee relationship than a friendship. I'm trying to learn as much as I can from her, about working with horses and with people.

"You're good at this," she finally says, smiling at me as she brushes out Horace's coat.

I look up at her, surprised. "At what?"

"Working with the horses. Talking to the guests. All of it."

My cheeks flush at the praise. "Thank you."

"George and Pamela don't usually hire new employees as wranglers, you know," she continues. I did not know that. "They usually hire all the newbies as cabin wranglers or activity guides their first summer and encourage them to learn about the horses if they want to be a wrangler.

But they were so impressed with your application, with your experience, that they made an exception this year."

"I didn't know, but I'm grateful they did." I smile. "I don't think I would have enjoyed cleaning cabins as much as this."

Leanne laughs. "Yeah, probably not." She's quiet for a few minutes, and I go back to picking out Pistol's hooves. She can be an ornery one, but I've come to love her, and she's usually the horse I choose to ride when I take guests out.

"What are you doing after this?" Leanne asks.

I shrug. "Having lunch."

"No, I mean after this summer. Are you going to keep working with horses?"

"Oh! Um . . ." I try to decide how to answer. The summer's winding down, and at this point I don't have a plan for what I'm doing next. I've been putting off thinking about it, but I know I can't for much longer. "I guess I'm not sure yet. I'll go home to my family's horse farm and figure it out."

"Your family doesn't have a position for you there?"

They do, and my parents—and Grammy—would be thrilled if I wanted to take a more active role in the farm. I know they'd love for me to take over the farm someday, keep it in the family for another generation, but they've never pressured me down the same path they took.

I do love working with the horses, if not the business side of things.

"They do," I finally answer. "If I want one."

Do I want one? When I was in college, I rarely had time to help at Steed Farm. This summer has reminded me how much fun it is to get to know the horses' personalities, train them, and take care of them.

I think I could be happy doing it long-term.

So, maybe that's my next move. Next time I'm within range of a cell tower, I'll talk to my parents and see what they think.

The thrill of anticipation in my chest gives me hope that I'm on the right track.

Chapter Twenty-Four

Jackson

I CAN'T BELIEVE I actually went horseback riding, or that I actually *liked* it. My horse was calm, even when I wasn't. The views were beautiful, especially when I turned to see the gorgeous wrangler behind me.

Then again, I'd probably like anything as long as Taylor's there. What other fears could I overcome with her by my side?

When she finally comes into the lodge for lunch, I'm one of the only people still here. Everyone else has eaten and wandered away again to their next activities.

I try to get Taylor's attention, but she's in some sort of daze. Her lips are pressed together, and her eyes are narrowed but unfocused, like her thoughts are far away. She grabs a tray and makes her way through the food line with an air of detachment.

She hasn't looked my way once or taken notice of anything around us in the lodge dining room. I know because I haven't been able to take my eyes off her. When Taylor stops in front of the drink dispensers, which happen to be next to the bin for dirty dishes, I jump up with my empty plate.

The heavy ceramic dish hits the bottom of the bin with a thud that finally gets her attention. Her head snaps up and she sees me, her eyes widening.

"Hey," she says. "I didn't think anyone would still be here."

"Just finishing up," I tell her. "But I could hang around for a while longer if you want company?"

Her mouth pinches to one side and I think she's going to say she wants to be alone, but then she puffs out a breath and smiles.

"That would be great. Maybe I could run something by you? An idea?" She narrows her eyes. "I had a revelation." She chuckles and murmurs to herself, "Two actually."

I take her tray as she fills a glass with cold water. "Sounds like quite the morning. Let's hear them. I don't have anywhere to be."

We settle into seats at one of the tables, and I place Taylor's tray in front of her. She takes two bites of salad before wiping her mouth with a napkin and turning her attention to me.

"I think I want to take over the farm," she says, propping her elbow on the table and resting her chin on top of her hand.

I lean back in my chair. "Your family's horse farm?"

She nods, biting her bottom lip with that hazy look in her eyes again. "It's an obvious answer to my problems, I know, but I'm pretty sure it's what I want. I could be happy making the farm my future."

For a second, I'm disoriented. While I'm glad she's landed on a direction that will make her happy after her job ends at B&B, I have this inexplicable resistance to the idea of Taylor being back in Florida. Across the country and far away from the only setting I've ever known her in.

Far away from me.

It's a selfish feeling because why shouldn't she go back to Florida and make a life there? It's her home, and it's not like I have anything to offer her instead.

She studies my face, and her eyebrows droop. "Do you think it's a bad idea?"

I clear my throat and shake away my thoughts. "No, of course not. It's a great idea. Why isn't it something you considered before?"

She bites her lip again in a way I find totally distracting. "It's been on my mind, but I felt like I wanted to experience something different before settling right into the same life I've always had. Plus, I was so focused on school these last few years that I forgot how much I love working with horses. Right now, my mom is the horse-farm manager, so she's in charge of the training and welfare of the horses. That's the job I would want. My dad is the overall manager, handling more of the business side of things. I don't want to do that, but I could probably hire someone to handle it for me once my dad retires."

Taylor frowns, and I'd love to know what thoughts are bouncing around in her head as she zones out again.

I nudge her arm to bring her back. "What was the second revelation?"

Her cheeks turn pink. "Hmm?"

"You said you had two revelations."

The blush deepens. "Did I? No, um, just the one."

She picks up her fork and starts eating, tidily closing the door on the subject.

The feeling of disorientation is back, like when I'm climbing and my hand slips. Even though I have three other points of contact with the rock, there's this spike of adrenaline as my body's center of gravity shifts. While climbing, I can usually regrip the hold quickly and everything settles. Even if I get totally off-balance, the belay system keeps me from falling or getting hurt.

I'm not sure I can deadpoint my way through this—there's not enough momentum for me to stabilize my hold while still stretching to make progress. And that's risky because there's no top rope for my heart.

Taylor is making plans for her life beyond this summer, plans that don't include me. Nor should they, but I can't shake the feeling that she's leaving me behind, and I'm in for a nasty ground fall.

EVER SINCE TAYLOR AND I held hands on our hike down Mount Washburn, our nightly meetups at the creek have been different. More tactile in the way I let my hand linger against her arm. Less careful in the way she drapes her legs over mine and we sink into each other.

We start each night at opposite ends of the rock, but always end up together, each of us inching closer to the other without making a conscious decision to do so.

It's difficult to cuddle when you're using a rock for a chair, but Taylor and I are getting pretty good at doing it anyway.

Friday night, we're so close together physically that I feel like she's surrounding me, her legs and arms and head all warming some part of my body, connecting us.

Mentally, though, she's been distant since lunch on Wednesday. I know she has a lot on her mind as she decides what to do about her future at her family's farm, but something else is there, too. Maybe this other revelation she didn't want to share with me.

Taylor's so forthright with everything else. She's been sharing her every thought and dream with me all summer, and it's made me greedy for more, even though I'm not being as open with her.

"Jackson," she hums, her throat vibrating against my shoulder in a way that makes me shiver.

"Hmm?" I turn my head and my nose nudges against the warmth of her cheek.

"Will you go on a date with me?"

I can't make sense of her question at first. Everything I feel for Taylor goes way beyond a casual date, though I've always intentionally kept that label away from the time we're spending together. *Friends*. That was the last official word on our relationship, but the mismatch between what it means and what we are is a canyon.

Carefully, I lean back to create some space between us. "Where is this coming from?"

A noise somewhere between a whimper and a laugh sounds in her throat. She gestures to the way we're wrapped in each other's arms. "It's coming from *this*." She sits up, pulling away from my side. "It's coming from everything that I'm feeling and that I think you're feeling too."

She breathes in a gulp of air and looks me in the eye. "It's coming from wanting to be honest about what we are to each other."

I can picture it all, then. Taylor and I holding hands as we walk down the street in Cody. Ordering dinner together in a restaurant and flirting across the table before sharing a dessert. Taylor dressed up for me, her hair curled around her face. Her smile. Her laugh. The warm blush on her cheeks in the glow of candlelight.

I want all of it, and so much more that I can't have. But maybe I can give us one date, one night when I don't have to hold myself so much in check, and I can simply enjoy her.

Slowly, I nod, still holding her gaze. “Yeah. Let’s go on a date.”

Chapter Twenty-Five

Taylor

EVEN THOUGH JACKSON AND I both work on Saturday, it's a short day after the guests leave and we prepare for a new group—the last group of guests for the summer—to come in tomorrow. An evening drive to Cody for dinner and a movie is easily manageable.

Jackson asks me to be ready to go by four. Even though *I* asked *him* out, he insists on making all the plans, and I'm dizzy with the anticipation of it all.

It's quarter to four now as I put the finishing touches on my outfit, Becca sitting cross-legged on my bed.

"Hair up or down?" I ask her.

Becca tilts her head, considering. "Down. You've got those pretty waves."

I comb my fingers through my hair and study the effect in the mirror. “Down it is.”

Picking out what to wear tonight was no easy task. I didn’t pack for this summer with the intention of dating. Most of my closet here at the ranch consists of jeans and Carhartt shirts. Grammy was the one who convinced me to slip a summer dress into my suitcase those many months ago. Boy, am I grateful for it now.

The dress is a blue chambray midi with thin straps over my shoulders and ruffles along the bottom hem. At home, I usually wear my espadrille wedges with this dress, but here I have only my sneakers and my boots to choose from.

I took some time cleaning up my boots, and they look cute enough paired with the denim style of the dress.

I’ve hardly worn makeup while I’ve worked here, either—some primer with sunscreen in it most days. Today, I took my time and applied a full face, though nothing glam or out of character.

It’s fun to get dressed up a little, and I grin, imagining Jackson’s reaction.

I twirl a strand of hair around my finger. I can’t believe I asked him out.

Okay, no, I can believe it. It was very on-brand for me, at least the old me. The amazing part was that I didn’t embarrass myself because he actually said yes.

After I realized that I’m in love with Jackson, all the wishy-washy touching and time spent together became tiresome. If we like each other, we should date. It’s as simple as that, and I’m not sure why we’re making it so complicated.

I understand there are obstacles. The distance, for one. In a little more than a week, I'll go back to Florida, and he'll be back to work in Colorado, after his Gannett Peak hike, of course.

And two . . . actually, I'm not sure I can think of any other challenges on my end. Jackson's got some walls up, sure, but I've already broken so many of them down this summer, and it's clear that the man behind them is worth the effort of the demolition.

A knock sounds on the cabin door, and Becca jumps up. "I'll get it! You finish up."

I'm ready to go, but I like the idea of Jackson waiting for me to make my grand entrance, so I accept Becca's offer.

Before long, I hear the rumble of Jackson's voice in the entryway, and my heart slams against my ribs.

Sucking in a deep breath, I take one last long look in the mirror. I wink at my reflection. "Here goes nothing," I whisper.

When I step into the hallway, Jackson stops talking mid-sentence. His mouth hangs open as his eyes rove over me from head to toe.

Becca grins behind him and slips out the front door.

"You look beautiful," Jackson finally manages to rasp out.

I preen under the influence of his praise, smoothing my dress against my thighs.

Jackson looks more handsome than he usually does, too. He's wearing dark jeans with a black button-down shirt with his sneakers. I grin thinking that he probably had the same struggle around footwear options that I did.

"Thank you," I tell him. "You look nice, too."

Flashing a bashful grin that makes my heart flip-flop in my chest, Jackson takes my hand and guides me out the door.

In the truck on the drive to Cody, an awkward silence hangs between us where there's usually open conversation or comfortable quiet.

Finally, Jackson clears his throat. "I'm nervous," he admits.

"About what?"

He tilts his head toward me with a doubtful look and a half grin.

I giggle. "Okay, I know. I'm nervous, too. But we've been hanging out all summer. Tonight doesn't have to be any different."

Keeping one hand on the steering wheel, he rubs his hand against his chin with the other. "It feels pretty different."

"Hey," I soothe, tugging on his right hand with my left, pulling it down from his face and twining our fingers. "It's just you and me, Jackson. It's going to be a good night."

He squeezes my hand and mutters under his breath. I catch every other word: *hope*, *night*, *perfect*.

I squeeze his hand back and try to distract him by telling him about a little girl on my trail ride yesterday. She was riding Mesa, a gray-and-white-dappled mare known for sneaking snacks whenever possible. All our horses wear grazing muzzles during rides to keep them from eating too many wildflowers along the way, but Mesa managed to wiggle out of hers.

The little girl thought it was hilarious when Mesa refused to move and instead gobbled big mouthfuls of grass and flowers.

By the time I finish the story, Jackson's shoulders are relaxed, and he's chuckling along with me.

He jumps in next with his own story about a boy at the archery range who tilted his bow at different angles to see where the arrows would end up. Jackson and Nick had to climb through a lot of trees to get all the wayward arrows back.

Before we know it, we pull into a parking lot behind an Italian restaurant, and Jackson parks the truck.

I reach for the door handle, but Jackson catches my wrist. "I'll get your door."

While I wait for him to come around the truck, I can't stop smiling. I'm finally on a real, intentional date with Jackson Hollis, and he's being adorably nervous and sweet.

It suddenly feels like everything I've been through—the painfully embarrassing crushes, the unrequited feelings, the string of bad first dates my senior year of college—has led me here, to this. To Jackson.

With only a week left in the guest season, a week until Jackson's much-anticipated hiking trip, we need to have a conversation about what happens next. If Jackson feels for me even a fraction of what I'm feeling for him, I need to know. We need to figure out how to navigate the distance to stay together—emotionally if not geographically for now.

The restaurant is dark with dreamy ambiance and the rustic, toasted scent of wood-fired pizza. A candle flickers low on the table between us as we look over our menus and place our orders.

After the server takes the menus, Jackson reaches across the table and wraps his hands around mine. His thumb gently, hypnotically traces a circle against my skin.

His eyes look almost liquid in the gleam of the candlelight, the brown richer and deeper than normal—like a dark chestnut—and his face half obscured in shadows.

He parts his lips as if he's going to say something, then ducks his head and clears his throat.

I nudge his foot with mine under the table, gently prodding. "What?"

He shakes his head, uncertainty and tenderness etched into the lines around his eyes. "This is exactly how I pictured it."

"This?"

"This date. You," he clarifies, smiling crookedly. "Being on a date with you."

Tilting my head, I lean closer. "Is that a good thing?"

"It's . . ." He chuckles. "Yeah, it's good."

I squeeze his hand and harness my outspoken tendencies, guiding them to the conversation I want to have. "Jackson, I like you."

That's an understatement, but with how forthright I've been about my general desire for a long-term relationship, I'm afraid that releasing the whole truth now will come across as a marriage proposal.

For a terrifying second, Jackson's grip on my hands fumbles, and his eyes flash with something sharp and unidentifiable in the low light. Then, his expression shifts into something determined and open, soft.

"I like you, too." His voice is scratchy with vulnerability. A wobble of bewilderment catches in his throat, as if the truth of his feelings for me has caught him by surprise.

I press my thumb into his palm like it will unlock a hidden door to his soul. "What's holding you back?"

He answers quickly. "Nothing." After a pause, he gives a more thoughtful answer. "Nothing anymore. I'm sorry it took me so long to get here this summer, but we have time. We'll be together all next week, after all."

I want to push further—dig into what he's thinking about a potential relationship, about maintaining this connection between us even after our time together in Wyoming ends—but the server arrives with our food and a flurry of polite, murmured niceties.

Jackson lets go of my hand to eat his pizza, and it feels like he's letting go of the thread of our conversation, too. I let him, for now.

WE FOLLOW UP DINNER with a movie at Cody's only cinema.

Jackson buys tickets to a new romantic comedy he knows I've been dying to see starring my favorite actress, Brianna Russo. She's famous for her gorgeous auburn hair and adorable comedic timing. Her characters are always crinkle-your-nose delightful, and her movies predictable in the best of ways.

"I know this is kind of cliché," Jackson says sheepishly as we settle into our seats with our popcorn and soda. "Dinner and a movie. But I was thinking that we've done so much this summer that was out of the ordinary, it might be nice to try something regular together, too."

I beam at him. "I like regular with you."

"I like everything with you," he murmurs as the previews start, blaring music through the theater and drowning out the last part of his words.

He flashes an apologetic smile and settles his hand on my thigh. It sits heavy and deliciously warm on my skin through the thin fabric of my dress. A tie holding us together, even when the anxiety in the back of my mind still worries our connection is only a slipknot, secure for now, but ultimately temporary.

I flip his hand over and plait my fingers through his, tightening the link between us.

The movie is light and sweet, but I have trouble keeping my focus on it. My imagination keeps skipping ahead to the end of the night, when Jackson will walk me to my door, and then . . . well, I have my hopes.

Jackson is such a gentleman. Will he hold back on kissing me on principle because this is technically our first date? We've spent so much time together, shared so much, and tiptoed around our feelings for so long that it doesn't feel like a first date. Time does strange things when you work and live around a group of people with no distractions for more than two months. George was right that we've all become a family.

Either way, I've waited long enough already for my first kiss.

Jackson squeezes my hand, and I startle, my face burning like he can tell what I'm thinking about in this dark theater. I don't look at him, just in case.

He nudges me with his shoulder, and I relent, turning to face him, certain he can read me like a book.

But he only gestures ahead with his chin. In the row in front of us, a few seats down from Jackson, two teenagers are, um . . . *affectionately* making out, totally in their own world.

I catch Jackson's eye and giggle.

He leans closer and whispers, "If any clothes come off, I'm out of here."

I clap my free hand over my mouth to block another round of giggles.

Jackson grins. "They could at least wait until they get back to his truck and make out in the back seat like civilized teenagers."

My shoulders shake with silent laughter as Jackson's smile widens. A muffled plop sounds from the row ahead as their bucket of popcorn falls to the ground in the shuffle of limbs and lips.

I snort, and even Jackson can't stop the pop of laughter that bursts out of him.

A woman two rows in front of us, closer to my side, turns and shushes us with an aggressive *shhh*. She points to the screen. I've lost the thread of the plot, but the two main characters are locked in a tender moment, tears dripping down the heroine's face.

For some reason, that makes me laugh harder.

Jackson pulls me into his chest and I laugh against him, my giggles absorbing into the soft creases of his neck. I could live right here for the rest of my life and be so happy.

This levity is the distraction I need. The change in tone that takes me from spiraling to silly.

The giddy energy sticks to us through the rest of the movie and most of the drive home. Jackson throws out a few more joking words he says describe me—"unsubtle" because of the way I drew attention to us in the movie theater, "uncouth" because I like the fake butter stuff on my popcorn, "unabridged" because he says with a grin that my stories are long-winded.

He's trying to tie in as many "un" words as he can, and I protest them all.

"I'll keep thinking," he teases.

The mood shifts again as we pull off the main road onto the B&B Ranch driveway. Not much longer now. If Jackson doesn't kiss me on my doorstep, maybe *I* should kiss *him*. Take the initiative for what I want instead of waiting for him to hand it to me.

The butterflies in my stomach are in full frenzy as we pass the bridge that leads to the stables. I peer out the window, my brain working to make sense of the commotion I see in the corral area.

"Stop!" I call out, and Jackson slams on the brakes.

"What's wrong?"

"Something's not right in the corral." I roll down my window to see better.

Leanne darts from the pole barn to the corral and catches sight of us over her shoulder.

"Taylor!" she shouts, her voice commanding. "We need your help! It's Pistol!"

I slip out of the truck, pausing only a moment to lean back through the window. "Sorry, Jackson . . ." I jerk my thumb behind me toward the corral. "Thanks for tonight. It was wonderful."

I blow him a kiss and bolt away, realizing with sharp disappointment that it's the only good night kiss Jackson and I will share tonight.

Chapter Twenty-Six

Jackson

THE NEXT MORNING BEFORE breakfast, Nick fills me in on the details about the crisis at the corral that derailed the end of my date with Taylor.

One of the horses—not Horace, obviously, because he would never—started kicking a couple of the other horses that she thought were crowding her. The wranglers, with help from Nick and Dennis, had to distract the horse with oats so they could separate her out into another pen.

"What will happen to the kicking horse? Will Leanne send her back to her home ranch?"

Nick shrugs. "I doubt it this close to the end of the summer. They'll probably keep her away from the guests and other horses. One of the wranglers will probably ride her for this last week."

I'm sure it's my lingering horse anxiety rearing up, but that does not sound safe. The thought of Taylor—or any of the wranglers, but especially Taylor—being near an unpredictable horse has my chest tightening.

Thinking about Taylor on our date last night loosens it back up. She looked gorgeous in that blue dress and her boots, her hair framing her face like it so rarely does while we're working. She always looks beautiful, of course, but knowing that she put extra effort into her appearance for me last night feels like that satisfying moment when I put my hand on the highest point of a formation and pull my body up until I can't go any further. It's that feeling of making it, of working hard the whole way up and being rewarded with an amazing view and sense of fulfillment.

She told me she likes me, and I said it back. The memory brings forward a whole new set of anxieties, ones I have trouble identifying as they weave their way through my stomach and up into my chest. Where are they coming from?

My reluctance around a committed relationship is because I'm not ready to settle down or give up my dangerous hobbies, right? That's what I've been telling myself.

Except now those reasons, logical as they are, don't seem to fit. The hesitation remains, but I can't figure out why.

Nick and I walk to breakfast at the lodge. It's a quiet morning, the staff getting ready for the last group of guests visiting B&B this summer.

Taylor's already sitting across from Becca eating scrambled eggs at one of the tables, so I plop my hat down into the chair next to her to claim it and squeeze the back of her neck as I walk past her chair to the food.

I wink when she looks up at me. "Mornin'," I drawl.

She blushes an adorable pink color like I hoped she would.

When I make it back to my seat balancing a plate and a glass of juice, Becca's gone. I scoot my chair closer to the table and busy myself slathering butter on my toast.

Taylor leans in and whispers, “You owe me a kiss.”

Between the heat of her breath on my neck and the mental image her statement stirs up, I nearly drop the knife.

“What?”

She giggles and leans back. “You owe me a good night kiss. I was robbed last night.”

Gulping, I reach for my glass of orange juice. I take a long drink to give myself a second to calm down.

I fully intended to kiss Taylor at the end of our date.

There was this whole plan to walk her through the trees to our rock by the creek. Tell her how beautiful and amazing and inspiring she is. And then kiss her.

I kind of feel like I was robbed, too, now that she mentions it.

Cynical though it may seem, I’m still not sure how we can sustain any sort of relationship with her in Florida and me in Colorado, but I want to try. For once, I push away logic and let myself sit in the terrifying and unpredictable realm of my feelings.

One thing is for sure: there’s no way I’m letting us go our separate ways next weekend without knowing how her lips taste.

After I drain my glass of juice, I flash Taylor a smile that’s cockier than I feel.

“Impatient.”

Her eyebrows pull together over her pretty brown eyes. “What?”

“Another word that describes you.”

She scowls. “I don’t like that one either.”

“I’ll keep thinking.” I tap my finger against my temple.

Now I have to come up with a new plan to kiss her that’s as romantic and perfect as she deserves for her first kiss. A weight sits on top of my heart, and I reflexively reach up and rub at my chest.

How perfect could it be when it's with me?

I'm no prize-winning catch. No clean send on a climbing route. No greased landing so smooth the plane passengers can't tell when we touch the ground. No golden ratio.

But against all odds, it's me Taylor wants, and I have trouble denying her anything.

TUESDAY IS ANOTHER EARLY morning for me. Nick and I are scheduled to take a family out to the river for fly-fishing, but with my Gannett Peak trip creeping up at the end of the week, I need to check my email to make sure I haven't missed any new information from the group leader.

I settle into the cozy armchair in front of the computer in the B&B library. As I navigate to my email and try to remember my password, I'm mentally making a list of what we'll need for fishing this morning.

The family is sweet—a mom and dad, son and daughter. The kids are somewhere between eight and ten years old. They spent their afternoon with me yesterday at the archery range, eager to learn everything.

And the way they interacted with each other was . . . I don't know. It was loving and gentle and fun. Of course it made me think of my mom. Our relationship had been like that, too. But it also made me think about Taylor—what it would be like to marry her, start a family with her, and take vacations together like the cute family visiting the ranch this week.

The images still make me feel like a weight is sitting on my chest—what if she gets sick like my mom did? What if one of the kids does? These worries are unexpected and sharp, and I wonder if they've been under the surface of my fears this whole time—but it's now maybe only a ten-pound barbell instead of twenty or thirty.

I can see a future with Taylor, specifically, and the idea doesn't scare me as much as thinking of a future with *any* woman would have at the start of the summer.

Finally, I type in the correct password—and in the nick of time because the website is about to lock my account for too many failed log-in attempts—and scan through the messages. Like I figured, I have one from the group leader for Gannett Peak, but it's nothing I don't already know. We're meeting on Saturday at a motel in Dubois for final checks and hopefully a good night's sleep before heading out on the trail first thing Sunday morning. It's a long four-hour drive from here to Dubois, so I'll need to leave the ranch right after breakfast on Saturday.

But not before I've kissed Taylor and gotten her contact information, I hope.

Another email catches my attention. It's from my dad, dated about a week ago. The subject line reads "Sorry." My stomach clenches as I open the message.

"Jack," he starts, and I already hate it because my dad knows I don't like him shortening my name. "I couldn't get a hold of you because you're in the mountains, but I swear it was an emergency, and I couldn't wait for you to get my voicemail and call me back. I had to borrow the money out of the trust. It was important, believe me. I'll pay you back once this new investment comes through."

There's more, but the words on the screen blur as my eyes defocus, and my hands drop to my lap.

Because . . . what the hell did I read? A part of my brain registers that my dad stole my money out of my trust fund that my dead mother left for *me*. The same woman he abandoned when she needed him most.

But another part of my brain—the foolish, stupid part that still hasn't learned its lesson—can't imagine it's true.

As the trustee of the funds until I turn twenty-five, my father does have access to the money, but it can't be legal for him to take it for himself. It can't be something that a father would actually do to his only child.

I scrape my fingers through my hair before grinding the heels of my hands into my eyes. I blink once, and then again, before focusing back on the screen to reread the words of this man who has disappointed me for the last time. Because I'm *done*. I'll hire a lawyer and let them deal with him from now on as I fight for my mother's money back.

My plans to buy a house this year are gone because now I don't have a down payment. I was looking forward to having a yard, maybe with a view of the mountains, and hoping to feel *settled* for the first time since before my mom got sick.

Inexplicably, as furious as I am with my father, I'm angry at Mom, too. At her forgiving and naive nature. *She* made him the trustee in the first place, after everything he did.

My heartbeat is loud in my ears, my chest so tight that my whole body shakes. I don't hear Nick approach until his hand is on my shoulder.

"You okay, man?"

I slit open an eye to look at him, and concern is painted all over his face. Nick's one of my closest friends, but if my own father can stab me in the back, what's stopping anybody else from doing the same?

I suck in a deep breath and sign out of the email account. Forcing my emotions back into their box, I turn to Nick with what I hope is a bland expression.

"Yeah, fine."

I'll get through this fishing trip this morning and somehow get through the next few days until I can forget everything again in the grueling relief of adrenaline on the mountain.

GOOD PLAN, EXCEPT THIS family, this innocent, kind, loving family I'm teaching to fly-fish in the Shoshone is breaking my heart.

Yesterday, I looked at them and saw the potential of a happy future with Taylor. I imagined it could be mine.

Today, I look at them casting their lines and laughing together, and I know it's not possible. My dad's betrayal has made it clear that a stable, loving family is not something I'm meant to have. I was fooling myself, thinking I could break a cycle he's ingrained in me so deeply.

I understand that this wound is still fresh, and I'm probably letting my emotions cloud my judgment, but I also feel the pressure of a ticking clock counting down the limited time Taylor and I have left breathing the same thin air.

If I don't make this decision now, it'll drag on in a soulless, frustrating long-distance *whatever* where I'll inevitably disappoint Taylor again and again.

Unlike with Nick, I don't have the same irrational fear that I shouldn't put my trust in Taylor. She's too good and too innocent. Too much like my mother, who trusted and loved with all her heart—even when someone didn't deserve it.

Taylor is sunshine. She's a cloudless blue sky I can see through for miles. She's the first snowfall of the season when the flakes are clean and cold. She's an untouched, wild waterfall frozen in place.

But I fly planes through clear blue skies. I stampede through freshly fallen snow, crushing it beneath my boots. I climb frozen waterfalls, cracking through their perfect surfaces with picks and crampons and ice screws.

Because here's the thing: I am my father. He was my first example of manhood, of being a husband and father. We even look the same. I can't bear the thought of breaking Taylor's heart the way my dad did to my mom.

What if I let Taylor down someday? What if I hurt her and abandon her when she needs me?

It's better for her if she never needs me to begin with.

Chapter Twenty-Seven

Taylor

As a group of guests and I splash across the creek on my favorite trail, one of the kids behind Pistol asks a question about the buildings we can see in the distance. I answer and then absently launch into a story about a boys' summer camp that's across the way.

Pistol snorts, and I pat her neck. After her temper tantrum the other night as Jackson and I were getting home from Cody, I've been keeping a close eye on her and her ornery mood.

Leanne and I have both checked her over, and I don't think there's anything physically wrong with her. She might be over the trail rides with guests and impatient to get back to her home ranch. I pat her neck again. *Soon*, I tell her in my head, *just a few more days*.

Unlike Pistol, I'd like to stretch these last few days so that they last another month or more. I'm not ready to go home yet. Not ready to leave the ranch or the mountains . . . or Jackson.

It's Thursday morning, and somehow, I haven't seen Jackson alone since Monday night. I frown as I think through the days. He didn't show at our rock by the creek Tuesday or last night. Hasn't sought me out at meals and always seems to be busy with guests when I've tried to seek him out.

I'm not above knocking on his cabin door—and will tonight if I can't catch him at dinner—but I'm sure there must be some simple explanation for his absence.

So much for all the time we were supposed to spend together this last week, though, and we still need to have a discussion about what comes next for us and how we're going to deal with being long-distance. We don't even have each other's phone numbers. There's been no need since our phones don't work out here anyway.

With these melancholy thoughts occupying my mind, I sigh, then refocus on the guests I'm supposed to be leading.

"When does school start again for you?" I ask the teenager a few horses back.

"A couple of weeks," she answers. "I'd rather stay here, though."

I bob my head in understanding. "It's a magical place."

The whole summer has been magical, and a part of me keeps waiting to be disappointed. Maybe the mountains are not as majestic as they seem. Maybe the air isn't as clear or the rides as peaceful. Maybe the man I love doesn't really like me back.

In the last stretch of the ride coming up the B&B driveway, I notice Pistol getting agitated again. She pins her ears back against her neck and shifts her weight.

I look behind us. The next horse is too close to Pistol's back legs for my comfort, especially with Pistol's tail swishing a warning like that.

"Hey, Clyde," I call to the boy behind me. "Go ahead and stop your horse, please. Pistol's getting a little agitated, and I want to give her some space."

From the back of the line, Becca hears me and pulls her horse around to my side. "We're almost back, but do you want to switch positions? Put Pistol in the back so she has a little more space?"

"Yeah, thanks."

I maneuver Pistol to the back of the line as Becca takes up the lead. The change seems to help; Pistol calms down for the rest of the ride back to the corral.

I hop down to help the guests dismount. Passing Pistol's reins to Leanne, I let her know what happened.

Leanne shakes her head. "I'll tie a red ribbon to her tail. I think this needs to be Pistol's last ride for the summer. I don't want to risk anyone getting hurt."

"Yeah, she's earned some rest."

Poor Pistol. As the guests are leaving on Saturday morning, I'll make sure to give her a little extra attention, maybe even a solo ride so she can have some exercise. Then she'll go home on Sunday, and I'll go home on Monday.

I DON'T SEE JACKSON at lunch at all. The fly-fishing outing he and Nick were leading this morning must be running late. Normally I'd wait for him, but I'm leading another trail ride for a different family this afternoon, and with Pistol out of commission, I need to choose and tack up a different horse.

At dinner, I look for Jackson again. He's already in the dining room at a table surrounded by guests.

He's smiling, but something feels off. The way he's picking at the dinner roll on his plate, maybe. Jackson usually inhales his food before I've had my first bite.

His table is full, so I park myself next to Becca instead. I'll grab him after dinner to check in.

I need to savor my last bits of time with Becca, too. We've already programmed each other's numbers into the contacts on our phones, and Becca teased coming to spend spring break with me in Florida next year. I tried to tell her that I don't actually live at the beach, but she didn't want to hear it.

Becca and I laugh our way through our pot roast and mashed potatoes until the guests start leaving the dining room for the saloon and their cabins.

Jackson's heading toward the saloon, too, so I tell Becca I'll see her later back at the cabin and run to talk to him, dropping my dishes into the soapy bin as I go.

"Jackson," I call, but he must not hear me.

I catch up to him and wrap my fingers around his arm. "Hey." I smile when he turns around to look at me. "I haven't seen you all day."

His expression is unreadable, except for it being obvious that he's not happy to see me. I drop my hand and frown.

"What's wrong?"

"Taylor, I can't talk to you right now. Here. I have saloon duty tonight."

The food suddenly feels too heavy in my stomach. "Okay," I respond numbly. Jackson is not acting like Jackson, and something is clearly wrong. My stomach clenches again, and the disappointment I've been expecting feels closer than ever. I need to talk to him alone and find out what's going on.

"Are you . . . is everything . . . will you meet me later tonight? By the creek?"

He searches my face, a storm in his expression I can't begin to decode without his help. He nods once, quickly.

One of the guests, an older woman with short white hair and tassels on her shirt, approaches to ask Jackson to play her in pool. After one last glance at me, he shifts his mouth into a smile that comes nowhere near reaching his eyes.

He offers the guest his elbow and walks away.

IT'S A COUPLE OF hours before Jackson makes it to the creek. I sit on the rock waiting for him, my knees tucked up under my chin and my arms wrapped around my legs.

Something terrible must have happened to have Jackson acting so strange. *Maybe it's the anniversary of his mother's death?* No, he told me that she passed away before high school graduation, sometime in the spring.

Maybe his Gannett Peak trip was canceled? That wouldn't explain why he's being cold toward me, though.

My worst fear is one I won't let myself articulate, not even inside my own head. It weighs on me all the same, though, solid and sharp on top of my chest.

Finally, as the sun is setting and the sky is starting to darken, he walks quietly through the trees into the clearing. His hands are stuffed into his front pockets, and his eyes are downcast.

"Hey," I say. Softly. Carefully.

He lifts his head to look at me, his eyes shadowed in the low light of dusk.

"Hey."

Hands still in his pockets, he slumps down onto the rock. Well, half on, half off, as if he can't sit far enough away from me.

Reaching across to him, the space feels like miles, even though in reality it's less than a foot. I set my hand on his arm. He flinches like I'm attacking him rather than trying to soothe him.

"What's going on, Jackson?" I fight to keep my voice steady. "What happened?"

I squeeze his wrist, and in one frenzied motion, he wraps me in his arms. My face smooshes against his shoulder, and his forehead rests against my hair. His hands move from my shoulders to my waist as he clutches me tighter. The embrace is anguished, frantic.

Wriggling my arms out from where they're trapped between us, I smooth my hands down Jackson's back, then up again. I run my fingers through the hair at his nape, scratching gently with my nails in an effort to settle him.

He stills, and the energy between us shifts into something heavy and heated. Slow and thick.

Jackson tilts his head so close that I can feel his breath on my forehead, warm and delicate. He brushes a kiss across my temple, then moves to place a lingering kiss on my left cheek. He shifts again, and my breath hitches as his lips hover over mine, an inch away for a moment. He continues to my right cheek and presses his lips to my skin, holding them there.

I lean into his touch, but he pulls away.

His face twists like he's in pain. His eyes are pure torment. And I'm lost, both in the sense of never wanting to let go of the thrill I felt at the touch of his lips but also confused.

He clearly wants to kiss me, regardless of what else might be going on in his head. I want him to kiss me.

"Jackson," I say, frustrated and breathy, "why won't you kiss me?"

Chapter Twenty-Eight

Jackson

In this moment, there's only one thing I want more than to kiss Taylor. She's here, right here, and her skin is warm, flushed, and comforting. I know her lips would be soft and willing. The strength I need to hold myself back right now is Herculean.

But the thing I want most is not to hurt her. I don't want to steal her first kiss and never speak to her again after this summer.

Selfishly, I also don't want to be someone she regrets. Someone who lets her down and leaves.

I've known it from the start, and every moment I've spent with her since has confirmed it. Taylor is not a woman to flirt with and kiss for a couple of months. Taylor is a woman who wants forever, and I can't give her that like she deserves.

My moment of weakness, of needy desperation pulling her into my arms, steels something inside of me. I know what I need to do.

I lean back, putting distance between us. "Taylor, the next man after me that you want to kiss will be your future husband. I know it. When you're old and have been married for seventy years, you're going to love to be able to say you've never kissed any man but your husband. I can't take that from you. From either of you. Your first kiss should be perfect, especially when you've waited this long for it."

The confusion and frustration on Taylor's face morph into a glare, and she pulls away even more. Relief and disappointment are a swirling cocktail in my chest.

"You don't get to decide what I want."

She's right, and ordinarily I wouldn't try to make a decision for someone else, but I have to be able to live with myself in the coming months and years.

I lift my arms helplessly, trying another tactic. "This is it for us, Taylor. On Saturday, I'm leaving B&B to meet up with my group for Gannett Peak. We won't see each other again."

We haven't talked about what the end of the summer means for us, at least not this overtly. Taylor's eyes widen at my blunt statements.

"But we can stay in touch. Outside of the wilds of Wyoming, there are such things as cell phones and the internet. Pretty sure they work in Boulder," she says bitingly.

I inhale a breath and then slowly exhale. "I think it's better if we don't."

Taylor reels back, her face wrinkled with confusion and hurt. "Why?"

I can't tell her about my father, about how like him I fear I am, so, instead of answering her question, I double down. "You've been a good friend this summer, Taylor, but—"

"*Friend*?" She hisses the word like an accusation. "Were we *friends* all those nights we sat here by the creek in each other's arms? When we held hands at Mount Washburn? When we were out on a *date* and you told me you liked me?" The pitch of her voice increases with each question until she's screeching in a tone that ripples with deadly quiet. "All the times we almost kissed?"

I close my eyes, whispering the lie as if that will save me from both seeing and hearing her reaction. "Yes."

She gasps, and I feel her move away as she stands up. I force myself to open my eyes and face her head-on.

It's a mistake, though, because her brokenhearted expression will be burned into my memory for the rest of my life. The way her eyebrows pinch to reveal two perpendicular lines centered on her forehead. The twist of her lips held tight in a drooping frown. The tears shimmering in her eyes.

"How can you say that?"

I grit my teeth. "Like I said, it's been fun hanging out, but I need to get back to the real world, and I suggest you do the same."

When she walks away, I've done my job, because the last thing she's thinking about now is kissing me. Killing me, maybe.

I know I'll remember this moment forever in heartbreaking detail, but I pray she forgets all about it. And me.

THE NEXT EVENING AFTER dinner, I get on the computer in the library to look up the phone number of my mom's lawyer, the one she worked with to set up the trust in the first place. Then I use the landline phone in the office to call and leave her a message explaining my situation. I let her know that I'll be unavailable for the next week, but I'll get in touch with her again when I'm back in Boulder.

That's all I can do for now.

Everything that's happened in the last couple of days, all the stress and pain, suddenly feels too heavy. I drop my head into my hands.

A throat clears from the direction of the office doorway, and I jolt up.

Nick. His expression is soft and pitying, like he knows too much.

"I, um . . . I overheard your phone call." He shuffles closer. "I'm so sorry, man. When did you find out?"

I stare at him, battling between two instincts, one saying to confide in my friend and the other urging me to push him away.

He takes another step toward me. "It was Tuesday morning, wasn't it? Before the fishing trip. I knew something was wrong. Why didn't you say anything?"

I shrug. "There's nothing you can do."

"Not about your dad or the money probably, but I can be a sounding board for you or listen as you vent. Find some stuff for you to punch."

I run a hand across my eyes. "I could punch some stuff." It might at least tide me over until I can lose myself in the adrenaline of Gannett Peak.

"Yeah, I bet. Let's head back to the cabin, and I'll see what we can do."

In the end, the pillows are too soft, the walls too hard, and the mattress too springy, so I settle for talking to my friend. I even tell him about running Taylor off last night.

He sucks in a breath through his teeth. "You're going to regret that."

I grunt in response.

"You will, eventually. I've seen the way you look at her, man. You're not going to find anyone else like her."

Oh, I'm aware. I won't regret pushing her away, because I did it for her sake. I'll feel the loss of her for a long, long time, though.

AFTER DARK, I WATCH out the window of my cabin as Taylor slips out the front door of hers, walking in the direction of our spot by the creek. Maybe it's habit, or maybe she knows I won't be there and wants some time to herself, but there's no way she's hoping to see me.

And still, I have to hold myself back from rushing outside and following her, wrapping her in my arms and inhaling the scent of her hair. Even when she disappears around a bend, I can't stop imagining finally kissing her like I've wanted to most of the summer.

But then what? She'll expect more from me than I'm capable of giving. And in a month or a year, eventually she'll need me, and I'll disappoint her. Just like my dad disappointed my mom and me.

Chapter Twenty-Nine

Taylor

I'M PATHETIC AND WEAK.

It's the only explanation for why I'm sitting out here on this rock by the creek again tonight, twenty-four hours after Jackson bucked me off like an angry bronco and dumped me in the dirt.

Even though I'm trying to convince myself otherwise, I'm waiting here for him. I'm hoping he'll reconsider and come back. Apologize and ask for a do-over.

I'd give him one in a heartbeat, even though he fed into my worst fear when he called us "friends" last night.

Something big must have happened to make him react the way he did, and I wish he would talk to me instead of shutting me out. He acted like a jerk last night—and yes, I went back to my cabin and cried for a solid half hour—but I know him well enough by now to know that he is not a jerk. Between his mother's death and his father's abandonment, Jackson has a lot of reasons to put up walls around his battered heart.

Maybe when he sees I'm not going anywhere, he'll stop pushing me away.

Jackson leaves in the morning, but I'm certain Nick will give me Jackson's phone number if I ask. I'll be hurt if he goes without saying goodbye, but it won't be the end of our friendship, even if that's all it will ever be.

After an hour by the creek, I give up and walk back to my cabin. I stop on the front porch and study Jackson's cabin next door. The lights are off and everything is quiet.

I open my door with a sigh, walking in on Becca sitting in the center of the floor surrounded by clothes.

I stop short. "What's going on here?"

Sheepishly, Becca peers up at me. "I thought I would get a head start on packing." She rubs the back of her neck. "Things kind of got out of control."

I can't help but laugh as I close the front door. Putting my hands on my hips, I survey the scene. "Looks like it. Let me help."

Like me, Becca's leaving on Monday after we help send the horses home on Sunday. Her fall semester at Texas A&M starts the following week.

My new job at Steed Farm kicks off that week, too. As I expected, my parents were thrilled when I asked them about training to take over the horse operations on the farm someday. I'm moving back home with them and starting my first full-time job at the place—*one* of the places now—I love the most. The salary is far too generous, but my parents insisted it's consistent with my experience.

Becca and I spend the next hour laughing and talking while slowly packing most of Becca's belongings into her suitcases and duffel bags.

I decide I'm going to relish these last few nights with her, trying to put Jackson out of my mind and heart to deal with later.

Still, I'm spinning lying in my bed trying to sleep. Jackson's leaving in the morning, and he hasn't said one word to me since our argument the night before.

SATURDAY MORNING, I'M UP early as usual. Becca and I feed the horses at the corral before stopping into the dining room to grab breakfast for ourselves.

I keep my eye out for Jackson, but I don't see him. I don't really expect to.

After breakfast, we return to the horses. Our main task today is to start mucking out the corral. We each grab a pitchfork and muck bucket and enter the fenced area.

The horses hardly pick their heads up from their grazing as I lug the muck bucket across the grass and start working.

From the corral, I have a perfect view of the gravel driveway leading from the staff parking lot to the main road. Pitchfork in hand, I slowly muck out the area by the water trough in between looking for a familiar black truck on the road.

I realize I'm staring instead of working when Nick approaches. He sets his boots on the bottom rail of the fence and lifts himself up until his arms hang over the top.

He greets me. "Hey."

I squint at him in the morning light. "Hey." I hesitate, then ask, "Has he left yet?"

Nick doesn't need to ask who I mean. He shakes his head, a somber look settling on his face. "Not yet. He's loading up his truck now."

My hands are frozen on the handle of the pitchfork; I'm not even pretending to work anymore. I nod and try to blink back my tears before Nick can see them.

He does anyway. "He'll change his mind." Nick's voice is gentle and soft, like the one I use when I'm trying to encourage an anxious horse to move.

I nod again. *I know he will. I'll* make *him change his mind.*

"Has he . . . did he say anything to you about what's going on? What got him so upset?" Jackson is obviously not talking about his feelings with me, but I hope he's confiding in someone.

Now it's Nick's turn to nod. "Yeah. Last night. He's having a hard time." His lips pull to one side, and he shrugs. "I think he needs some space."

I clear my throat, the nervous tic reminding me of Jackson. "That's what I figured, too."

Nick fishes his phone out of the pocket of his jeans. "Here," he says, swiping at the screen. "What's your number?"

I rattle off the digits as Nick's fingers peck away at the screen. When he finishes typing, he looks up at me.

"Once I have service, I'll text so you have my number, too. You won't lose contact with Jackson, even if that's what he thinks needs to happen right now." He pauses as if something new has occurred to him. "Unless *you* don't want to stay in contact with *him*."

"I do," I say quickly. "I was going to ask you for his phone number."

I hear a squeal behind me and turn to see Pistol scuffling with one of the other horses again, blocking her from a pile of hay.

"Pistol," I warn in a low voice. She swishes her tail in a way that lets me know she hears me.

I turn back to Nick.

"Anyway, thanks for this." I smile at him, shy and appreciative. Nick is one of Jackson's closest friends, so it's nice to know he's on my team. Gratifying to know that I'm not the only one who thinks Jackson isn't acting like himself.

Nick waves a hand. "I'll see you later."

My eyes blur on his form walking away as I zone out, lost in my thoughts. *Will Jackson find me to say goodbye before he leaves? Should* I *seek him out and force a conversation?*

But no, Jackson talked to Nick, and Nick said that Jackson needs space. It won't do any good to corner him.

I shake my head, and my vision clears in time to see Nick look back at me over his shoulder. His eyes widen, his expression stunned as he shouts.

"Taylor! Look out!"

Chapter Thirty

Jackson

MY SIDE OF THE cabin is almost empty. I've packed my things into two suitcases, with everything I need for my Gannett Peak trip in my pack. Loading it all into my truck, I pull the cover over the bed so my stuff will stay safe and dry while I'm hiking and climbing.

I check my watch. It's time to go, but leaving B&B, maybe for the last time, hurts. I set my hands on my hips and look around.

It's quiet. Almost everyone is seeing the last batch of guests off in the lodge or working down at the pole barn to get the horses ready to go home.

Nick and I said goodbye this morning, and I talked to nearly everyone else last night.

I probably shouldn't say goodbye to Taylor. I should let it be. And anyway, she's busy with the horses.

The creek babbles behind me through the trees, and I know I still need to find a way to say goodbye to the ranch.

Reaching through the open window of the truck cab, I grab my blue ball cap from the passenger seat and tug it onto my head. Then I take the familiar path to my spot by Libby Creek.

Our spot, my brain unhelpfully reminds me. I'm trying my best not to think about Taylor.

But of course, once I'm sitting on the rock alone, all I can think about are the times I sat here with her. Talking and teasing. Flirting and falling.

I stare into the water running over the stones and think again that I'll never meet anyone else like her as long as I live, and I'll never get the memories of this summer out of my mind.

Nick was right. I'm already regretting leaving things with Taylor the way I did. We never even exchanged phone numbers.

Abruptly, I stand. *What am I doing?* I can't leave without some sort of contact information or plan to see Taylor again.

Why did I think ending things with her was a good idea?

I have to find her, now, before I go. I have to talk to her and make sure that when I'm done with this climb, I have some sort of possibility of talking to her again or even seeing her again. Maybe she'll still want to be friends, even if I'm wary of giving her anything more.

Then, two things happen at the same time that divert me from that plan.

First, Nick rushes into the clearing, shouting my name.

Second, the loud, out-of-place sounds of a helicopter flying low overhead have me looking up, stunned. It's a black medical transport helicopter.

Nick grabs my shoulder. "I've been looking for you everywhere!" I focus on his face, and it's panicked, scared. His eyes are wide, and he's breathing heavily.

Before he says anything, I can already guess why he's here. I feel it in my gut, and I want to cover my ears like if I can't hear him, nothing happened, and she's okay.

"It's Taylor," Nick pants. "A horse kicked her, and it looks bad. They're airlifting her to the hospital in Cody."

He shouts the last part after me as I race through the trees and down the path to the pole barn.

I burst through the gate at the same time the paramedics strap Taylor to a bright orange plastic board. I try to push my way through the crowd of my coworkers to get to her, but I'm stopped by hands on either side of my arms, holding me back.

"Stay back, son," George warns.

All I can think about is getting to her, making sure she's okay. I struggle against George's grip, trying to break free, but he holds fast.

"Taylor!" I shout. I see her head move, twitching slightly toward my voice. The board they have her on has two blue foam pads that bracket either side of her head and hold her in place.

"Calm down, now," George soothes, his voice soft and even. "They'll take care of her. We have to let them do their jobs."

I watch impotently as the paramedics lift the board with Taylor on it and carry it toward the helicopter. George keeps a tight hold on my arms until she's loaded up and the helicopter takes off.

I feel George's hands loosen, and I pull away, running toward the empty field, standing powerless as Taylor disappears into the sky.

"Taylor!" I shout again, because it's all I can do.

Pamela and Nick approach me on either side, and Pamela sets her hand on my shoulder. "It's okay, now, darlin'. They'll get her to the hospital and take care of her."

"The hospital," I repeat to myself.

I have to get to the hospital!

I'm moving on pure adrenaline as I tear my truck keys out of the pocket of my jeans and run for the parking lot.

I hear someone calling after me, but I ignore them, too focused on getting to Cody. Getting to Taylor.

The scenic, meandering drive down the mountain from B&B to Cody has never been so unbearable. I pass RVs and horse trailers on the two-lane road without bothering to notice if the center line is dotted or solid.

I can't lose Taylor.

The thought is sharp and clear. A conviction. A timeless truth that an hour ago I was actively and knowingly choosing to defy. As much as I'm out of control now careening down this mountain road, I was out of my mind then, thinking I could ever survive without her in my life.

Halfway there, I realize I should have stopped for a minute and gotten some information before leaving the ranch. Find out exactly what happened. Was she conscious? Coherent? Did the paramedics say anything about her condition?

Does she hate me?

The question urges me to push down harder on the gas pedal. It's the least amount of time the drive to Cody has ever taken me, and it's still too long.

Somehow, I make it to the hospital in one piece. I park my truck and barrel through the front doors.

Inside, the quiet and sterile brightness knocks me down a peg. My throat closes as memories slam into me: my mom, emaciated and weak in her hospital bed, or bald sitting for chemotherapy. I see the teenage version of myself, wandering the hospital halls, overwhelmed and grieving. Alone.

I take a breath to steady my nerves before I approach the desk.

"Excuse me," I say, my voice sounding cracked and scared even to my own ears. "I'm looking for a patient that came in by helicopter, maybe half an hour ago. Taylor Steed-Gallagher?"

The desk clerk is an older woman with tawny skin and curly gray hair. Her dark eyes assess me, and I can only imagine what she's seeing. Pale face. Disheveled hair. Panicked eyes.

"You'll have to take a seat," she tells me, her tone firm and kind. "I'll let the nurses know you're here, and they'll come talk to you when they have any information to share."

I stand frozen to the spot, frustrated to come all this way, be in the same building as an injured Taylor, and not be able to go to her.

"Go on," the clerk urges, her eyes soft, as she points to the waiting area on the far side of the room. Several of the chairs are occupied, family and friends of other patients sitting rigid and restless. I guess I need to join them.

"Sit there. They'll come get you when she's able to have visitors," she tells me again.

All of a sudden, I'm so tired. The adrenaline has left my system, and I just want to see Taylor and make sure she's okay. Hold her hand. Tell her I'm never leaving her side again.

Resigned, I shuffle over to the waiting area and sit.

After an hour of restless pacing and scrolling through social media past all the content I hadn't really missed over the last three months, my phone vibrates with a call. The number for the ranch's landline flashes on my screen.

I glance around the room. A few other people are waiting, and while I don't want to disturb them with my phone call, I want to miss someone coming by to talk to me about Taylor even less. I don't take the call outside.

When I answer, Pamela's relief-filled voice echoes in my ear. "Jackson. Are you safe? Did you make it to the hospital?"

"Yeah, I'm—"

"Oh, honey. You tore out of here so quickly we were afraid you'd crash into the Shoshone."

"No, I made it. Listen, how was Taylor when the paramedics got there? What did they say? No one's told me anything here."

"Pistol was picking fights with another horse again, and Taylor got in the way. She was awake, but the paramedics were worried about broken ribs and internal bleeding. The doctor called us a few minutes ago since we're her emergency contacts for the summer. She's in surgery now. I gave them her parents' phone number and told them you were probably in the waiting room."

I rub my forehead. I didn't think about calling Taylor's parents. Not that I would have any way of getting in contact with them.

"Thanks, Pamela."

"Of course, honey." She pauses like she has something else to say but isn't sure if she should.

"Anything else?" I prompt warily.

"Well, I've watched you and Taylor together this summer, and it's obvious you care about each other, so I think you're right where you need to be. But, honey, aren't you supposed to be driving down to Dubois today for your hike?"

Gannett Peak. I flip my wrist until I can see the face of my watch. I should be halfway there by now. From the moment I heard that helicopter, I'm not sure I thought of my trip once. There was no decision involved, only the fully fledged conviction of where I needed to be.

"Yeah. I was supposed to, but I'm not going anywhere now."

Pamela chuckles. "I didn't think you would be. I'll let you know if we hear any more updates, and you do the same, okay?"

I rub my hand across my eyes. "Will do. Talk to you soon."

We hang up, and I stand, putting my hands on my hips and stretching out my lower back. I'm not leaving the waiting room, but I have a phone call to make and a deposit to forfeit.

Chapter Thirty-One

Jackson

EVENTUALLY, A WOMAN DRESSED in maroon scrubs comes into the waiting room and calls, "Jackson?" She smiles at me, and I jump out of my seat.

"Yeah, that's me."

"Taylor's out of surgery and doing well. She'll probably be asleep or out of it from the medication the rest of the day, but we were able to talk to her briefly after the surgery. When we told her you were in the waiting room, she asked for you. She was a little confused, but that's to be expected in her condition."

The words bounce around my brain a few times before I can make sense of them. *Taylor wants me?* Even after everything I said to her the other night, she's glad I'm here? If she asked for me, even in a post-surgery haze, maybe she doesn't hate me after all. Maybe I haven't screwed this up too badly.

"She asked for me?" I ask, wanting to make sure I'm getting it right.

The woman smiles again. "She did. If you follow me, I'll take you to her room."

She leads me through a maze of hallways, stopping in front of an open door. I peek warily through the doorway.

The bright hospital room is a horribly familiar sight. A window that looks out onto the parking lot. Cabinets low along one wall with a flat screen TV mounted above them. A door leading to what I assume is a bathroom. An armchair against a wall covered in ports and buttons and outlets of various colors. A rolling cart with a mouse and keyboard on it, computer monitor hanging above.

My chest tightens, and I flashback to my mom. Of course I do. How much time did I spend with her in hospital rooms like this in those last few months? Nights that I drove her to the ER and then dozed on a sleeper chair next to her bed before waking up to go to school the next morning. Afternoons I cried in her empty room while she was having some procedure or another done and then washed my face in time to greet her with a forced smile when she returned.

I shake my head to bring myself back to the present, to see the reality of the room in front of me instead of flickers of those that haunted me in the past.

In the center of the room is an uncomfortable-looking hospital bed on wheels, Taylor on her back under the blanket, tubes curling up from her arm and connecting into an IV pole.

Her eyes are closed, her face pale in the harsh fluorescent lighting. She looks small, drowning in the hospital gown and covers.

I swallow and shore up my courage to perch on the edge of the armchair next to the bed. Resting my elbows against the scratchy blanket, I clasp my hands together and tuck them under my chin. Taylor's chest rises and falls as she breathes, and I follow the motion with my eyes, letting it soothe my nerves.

Except for nurses coming in to take her vitals or make her blow into a spirometer, Taylor sleeps the rest of the day with me sitting by her side.

I call the ranch at one point to give everyone an update. George says they're all praying for her.

At nine o'clock that night, a nurse finally makes me leave. Nowhere else to go, I drive the hour back up to B&B.

EARLY THE NEXT MORNING, I'm back in my truck heading toward Cody. I feel better after a shower and some rest—plus Chip's homemade breakfast—but there's still this dull grasp of panic squeezing my chest.

I stop at a florist shop to pick up a bouquet of wildflowers, but then realize the hospital probably has a policy against fresh flowers in the ICU. I wander around the shop trying to find something else to bring, something that will cheer her up and remind her of this summer.

Turning the corner of an aisle, I see the perfect gift: a bison stuffed animal. Taylor loves seeing the fluffy cows both at the ranch and in Yellowstone, and they're unique out here in the West, so it's meaningful to her time here.

I'm more confident entering the hospital today. Less encumbered by ghosts from my past. The stuffed bison in my hands keeps me grounded and my mind on Taylor.

When I get to her hospital room I stop short, a bit of that confidence slipping away. Two women I don't recognize are on either side of Taylor's bed. They don't notice me coming in, so I clear my throat.

"Hello," I choke out awkwardly.

Both women turn to me.

Well, wait. I squint. I guess I do recognize them.

The older woman has the same nose as Taylor and the same light brown eyes. And the younger woman, too: the same eyes, and hair a smidge lighter and shorter than the hair draped over Taylor's sterile white pillow. This must be Taylor's mother and grandmother.

"I'm Jackson . . . Hollis. Jackson Hollis," I say, fumbling over how to explain myself. "I'm—"

Grammy's eyes light up. "You're the boyfriend."

My whole face gets hot. "I'm not . . . I don't think . . ." I take a deep breath. "Well, I hope to be, anyway. If she'll have me. How is she this morning?"

Mrs. Steed sighs, rubbing her hand across her forehead. "She's stable. The doctor says that no internal organs were damaged, but the blunt force tore open blood vessels, which led to some internal bleeding. She cracked a couple of ribs, too. But the doctor said that she'll start being more responsive today as they dial back her medication."

I swallow. "Okay. That's . . . that's good."

Grammy grins. "I remember the first time I got in the way of a horse's hoof. I didn't need to go to the hospital, but I had a bruise the size of a grapefruit on my thigh for weeks."

Mrs. Steed grabs Grammy's arm. "Oh, do you remember the time that bronco threw you and broke your wrist?"

"Oh yes." Grammy nods. "Or how you hobbled down the aisle at your wedding because Blazer stepped on your foot the week before?"

The ladies laugh, and I stare at them, unblinking. They're talking about their horse-related injuries like fond memories.

My expression must give away my bafflement because Grammy and Mrs. Steed tuck away their smiles when they look at me.

"I'm sorry, Jackson," Mrs. Steed begins. "In our line of work, we tend to see these kinds of incidents as occupational hazards. I don't think there's anyone at our farm who hasn't suffered some kind of injury working with the horses. I hope you don't think we sound callous."

I mean, I did think so, a little bit.

Grammy jumps in. "Hearing about Taylor's accident scared us enough that we got on the first flight to Wyoming, but now that we know she's going to be fine, well, it's almost like she's officially joined our ranks. It's a badge of honor."

I hate the idea that Taylor lying in a hospital bed is any kind of honor, but admittedly, my climbing buddies and I have a similar attitude about our injuries from a good climb. Bleeding knuckles, bruised shins, and even losing toenails are considered evidence we're pushing the limits of our bodies.

"No, it's fine. I think I understand." I hesitate but decide to try being more open about my feelings. I clear my throat. "But it was scary watching the helicopter fly her away from the ranch and hard sitting with her yesterday without knowing how she was doing."

Grammy puts a hand to her chest, and Mrs. Steed rushes over to me, folding me into a hug. I sink into it, letting her arms provide the comfort I so desperately need.

"I'm so sorry, sweetie. We're being insensitive." She squeezes me tight, and then me lets go, holding onto my shoulders as she studies my face. "Taylor will be fine. She'll be sore for a while, for sure, but she's young and healthy. The doctor is confident she'll be out of the hospital within a week."

I swallow past the lump in my throat. "A week?"

Grammy comes forward. “You know what? Let’s take a break. Taylor’s dad went down to the cafeteria, and he’s been gone a while. Why don’t you come with me to find him?”

I hold up the stuffed animal stupidly. “But I have this.”

Mrs. Steed takes it from my hand. “Oh, what a sweet buffalo! You can give it to Taylor when she wakes up. I’ll set him over here in the meantime.” She puts Taylor’s gift on one of the chairs. I don’t have the energy to correct her use of the term *buffalo*.

Grammy takes my hand and pulls me from the room. “Let’s get some coffee. Have you had breakfast?”

I nod my answer and follow Grammy down the hallway through the lobby and across to the hospital cafeteria.

We don’t run into Mr. Gallagher, but Grammy steers me to a table and deposits me there anyway. She fixes two cups of coffee and brings them over, handing one to me.

Sitting down in the seat next to me, she takes my free hand in hers. “I know this isn’t the best introduction, but I’m glad to meet you, Jackson. It’s obvious you care about my granddaughter, but I feel like there’s another layer to your concern?” She watches my face carefully. “Or maybe several layers. Would you like to talk about it?”

At the beginning of the summer—heck, even a few days ago—I would have brushed off her offer to talk. I would have shoved my anxiety and grief and anger down below the surface of my “friendly guy” personality.

I don’t want to be that guy anymore. Taylor unlocked something in me this summer. She helped me want to enjoy life again, to find happiness in the beauty around me and delight in the little things. I need to deal with the negative emotions I’ve bottled up to make room for the positive ones I want to feel.

I know it won't be easy, though. I can start here with a conversation with Taylor's grandmother.

I clear my throat miserably. "We, uh . . . we weren't on the best of terms when she had her accident. I let her think I *don't* care about her. I need her to know I do, but . . ."

Squeezing my eyes shut, I consider how to explain all my swirling thoughts and feelings. Grammy waits patiently for my explanation.

"But I'm not good enough," I finally say. I pause, then continue, sharing an explanation. "Even though we lived in Colorado, my mother loved the beach. Every summer we'd drive to San Diego and go to this one beach that always had shells washed up on the sand. She'd collect the most beautiful, perfect shells she could find and show me how they spiraled, getting wider at the same rate they got longer. A logarithmic spiral, the golden ratio.

"After she . . . she died, I went back to that same beach and scattered some of her ashes there. I found a huge whelk shell, the most perfect I'd ever seen. It was a sign from her, I'm sure of it."

I take a deep breath. "Anyway, my mother was perfect and beautiful and happy like that. Taylor reminds me a lot of her. But I'm not. I'm more like . . . well, I don't know if I can be what she needs me to be."

Grammy ponders my words for a moment, her lips pinching to the side in an expression that's so like Taylor my chest aches. I appreciate that she doesn't rush to fill the silence with empty reassurances.

"Well, sweetie," she finally says, "your mom sounds like she was a smart lady. But being from the mountains and not the beach, there's a bit of information she might have forgotten to mention about shells."

"What's that?" I ask.

"They don't have to be perfect to be beautiful. We collect them all. If you're determined to be your best for Taylor, to love her how she needs to be loved, that's enough. *You're* enough. After all, you're here at this hospital, aren't you? You've been here from the beginning, waiting to do whatever she needs."

I never used the word *love* when I told Grammy about my feelings for Taylor, but she figured it out anyway.

I love Taylor.

I tried hard to deny it all summer, but I've been a goner from the beginning. She hustled me out of my heart at the same time she hustled me at cards.

The idea that I don't need to be perfect to love Taylor settles into my soul. Shells with perfect spirals are beautiful, but even the broken ones are worth keeping. *I'm* worth keeping.

"Thanks, Grammy," I say softly. Then when I realize what I've said, my face warms. "I mean, Mrs. Steed." I stumble over the words.

I've been calling her *Grammy* in my head, but that doesn't mean I have a right to use Taylor's familiar nickname for her grandmother out loud.

Mrs. Steed—Grammy—pats my shoulder. "That's all right, sugar. You can call me Grammy." She winks. "I have a feeling you'll be around for a while."

I can only hope.

Chapter Thirty-Two

Taylor

Snatches of familiar voices break through to my groggy brain as I wake up. I have fleeting, slippery memories of where I am and what happened, but I'm having trouble holding on to them, making sense of what's in my head.

Like the voices. They sound like my family—my mom and dad, Grammy—but my family is in Florida, and I'm in Wyoming. I remember that much.

The voices that sound like my family get louder, and I blink my eyes open.

It *is* my family! And I'm in a hospital room with what feels like a tube up my nose, a throat drier than the desert, and worst of all, a searing pain in my stomach.

I groan, and my parents rush over.

"You're awake!" My mom smiles down at me. I try to sit up, but that pain in my stomach is too much. Mom presses a button near the bed that tilts the mattress up with me on it so I'm in a reclining position.

"Mom," I scratch out. "What . . ."

She pats my shoulder. "You don't need to talk, Taylor. Just rest. You were in an accident at the ranch. Do you remember?"

My brain supplies the memory. I was talking to Nick about Jackson, not paying attention to the horses. Then I turned around, and there was Pistol, backing into me, my stomach receiving the kick meant for Mesa.

After that, the picture gets blurry. I get vague snippets of helicopter blades, beeping heart monitors, and a dream where Jackson leans over me, concern in his expression.

"You're here." My voice is hoarse, and I swallow, feeling the tube at the back of my throat.

"Of course we are! You're in the hospital. Where else would we be?" My mom tsks. "And Jackson's around here somewhere, too. I'm sure he'll be back any minute."

I don't remember hitting my head, but maybe I have a concussion, too? Because I can't seem to make sense of that statement.

"Jackson's not here," I protest weakly.

I would give almost anything if he were. If I could see his face and hold his hand through this pain, but I know he's not hanging around the hospital for me.

The door to my room opens. I expect it to be one of the nurses, but it's a much more familiar form that fills the doorway.

It *is* Jackson. He's here, in rumpled joggers and a T-shirt, his hair messy as if he's been running his hands through it.

When he sees me sitting up in bed, his eyes go wide with surprise and relief. He shoots me an easy smile that looks too wobbly to be genuine.

"You're awake."

"Jackson?" I rasp.

A thought occurs to me, and I try to process it, but my head still feels fuzzy. "What day is it?"

"Sunday." Grammy helpfully supplies the word that's key to opening my memory.

"Sunday." I stare at Jackson. "Your trip . . . What about Gannett Peak?"

Jackson shrugs, looking uncomfortable as he takes a few steps closer. "I didn't go. I don't care about Gannett Peak."

"Yes, you do!" I squeak out. "It's all you've talked about all summer."

Jackson runs his hand through his hair and clears his throat. "It might be all I talked about, but all I thought about was you. I care about *you*."

He says it so earnestly that I wonder if maybe I'm still unconscious and this is a dream.

My parents glance between me and the door with unsure expressions.

"Why don't we give you two a minute?" Mom suggests, pushing my dad out of the room.

Grammy waves her away. "Well, hold on now. Things are starting to get interesting."

"Mom!" my mom says sharply.

"All right, all right. I'm coming," Grammy grumbles. She winks at Jackson before stepping out into the hall.

"You do?" I ask as Jackson shuffles closer.

My throat is sore, but this is a conversation worth having, I suspect.

Jackson's ears turn red. "I do."

Before I can finish processing his words, Jackson closes the distance between us. Bending over me and ducking his head, he brushes a sweet, chaste kiss over my lips.

My first kiss. *Wait! My first kiss?* With my lips dry and a tube up my nose while I'm lying in a hospital bed?

"That doesn't count!" I rasp over my scratchy throat.

Jackson gives a resolute nod. "It counts," he says. "Both as your first kiss and as a promise of more kisses to come. Taylor, I . . ." His face takes on a pained expression, and he combs his fingers through his hair. "I've been an idiot. I thought I wasn't ready for a serious relationship, and it was obvious to me from the start that's what you deserve. I thought to be worthy of you I'd have to be more . . . well, I don't know, just more, better. Perfect, I guess.

"And I thought your first kiss needed to be perfect, too. Perfect setting. Perfect man. Now, I realize that I was wrong. I don't need to be perfect to love you or to accept your love."

I gasp silently, scrubbing my hands over my cheeks to wipe off the tears. "Love?" I ask, barely audible.

Jackson, still standing next to the bed, lifts his hands in a helpless gesture. "I love you, Taylor."

That was a long speech, and this is a lot of information for me to process while I'm still half groggy on pain medication, but I register those four words loud and clear.

Jackson loves me.

"I love you, too." I sniffle.

A cautious smile takes over his face. "Yeah?"

I nod. "Yeah. I thought it was pretty obvious."

Jackson's smile dims. "You aren't mad at me? For those things I said by the creek?"

I yawn and blink my heavy eyelids. Our weighty conversation has drained what little energy I have. "I'm too tired to be mad at anyone right now. Ask me again in a few days. Maybe I'll be mad at you by then."

Jackson laughs. "I'll look forward to it." He leans over to brush a soft kiss against my forehead. "Rest now. I'll be here when you wake up."

I close my eyes, hearing him shuffle toward a chair in the corner of the room. For some reason, the sound fills me with an overwhelming feeling of safety and reassurance. I blink my eyes open again.

"Jackson," I call in a weak voice.

He turns. "Hmm?"

"My first kiss was perfect," I tell him with as much of a smile as I can find. "Because it was with you."

I never needed it to happen at Artist Point or under the stars by a beautiful creek. I just needed it to be Jackson.

By Tuesday afternoon I've moved out of the ICU into a regular hospital room, and I'm much more alert, though my conversation with Jackson still feels like a fever dream. Every time I've woken up between his speech and today, I've been surprised to see him here, and he's had to remind me that yes, he's here. No, he's not going to Gannett Peak. And yes, we're officially in love.

The first time I wake up with a clear head, I almost pretend I'm still out of it, so he'll go through it all again. I'm not sure I'll ever get tired of Jackson telling me he loves me.

What I *am* tired of is being in the hospital with everyone fussing over me. Each time the nurse comes in to help me stand and take a few steps around the room, I feel like I have a whole army of overprotective soldiers ready to dive forward and catch me at my slightest wobble.

My stomach and ribs hurt. I'm not allowed to eat or drink. I'm stuck in this hospital room after being outside most of the last three months. And I want to go home.

That last one is tricky because I know that going home to Florida means leaving Jackson. We have quiet, earnest conversations about how we'll make a relationship work long distance. We're both committed to it, to each other, but the thought of being apart when we've finally owned our feelings makes my heart hurt almost as much as the incision on my stomach does.

Wednesday morning, Dr. Freeman, who performed my surgery, stops by my room to give us an update. As has become our usual circumstances, my parents are sitting on a couch by the window with Grammy next to them in a sleeper chair. Jackson has another chair pulled up next to the bed.

The support is nice, but there are a lot of people in this small room.

Dr. Freeman must think so, too, because she stops short inside the door and surveys all the faces before addressing her update directly to me.

"Taylor, everything is looking great. If we can get you up and walking the halls starting today, I'm confident we'll be able to discharge you on Saturday."

My parents pepper Dr. Freeman with questions, including when I might be cleared to fly so we can go home.

She grimaces. "I won't clear you to fly for at least three weeks, and only if your recovery continues to go smoothly. I'm sorry, Taylor. There are too many risks involved due to the pressurized cabin and low oxygen levels, not to mention the jostle of the airport and boarding a plane." She gives me a sympathetic smile. "I can have the hospital concierge recommend some extended-stay hotels in the area."

After Dr. Freeman leaves, my family buzzes as we try to figure out the logistics of me staying in Wyoming another three weeks until I can fly home.

We decide that Dad and Grammy will fly home on Sunday after I've been discharged and settled somewhere else—we're still trying to figure out where—while Mom stays with me in Wyoming.

Jackson's quiet. Of course, I expect he'll need to head home to Colorado sometime soon. He does have his job waiting for him in Boulder, and apparently a legal fight with his dad to try to recover his stolen money. I know he won't be able to keep sitting around with me for the next three weeks.

Abruptly, Jackson stands, and we all turn to look at him. His ears turn red, and he clears his throat. "I have an idea." He holds up his phone. "Give me a few minutes." With that, he walks out of the room.

My parents and Grammy have been staying in a hotel near the hospital since they arrived in Cody, but Jackson's been driving back and forth from B&B. It's obvious he's exhausted, though he tries to hide it.

Fifteen minutes later, Jackson's back with a grin on his face. "Got it."

I blink at him. "Got what?"

"A place to stay. George and Pamela aren't moving out of their apartment up at B&B until late September. They said we can stay at their Cody house as long as we need to."

Mom stands. "Oh, that's so generous of them!"

It is generous, and very like George and Pamela, but my brain has snagged on a different detail from Jackson's announcement. "We?" I ask.

Jackson's smile falters. "I thought I would stay, too, until you leave." He looks between me and my mom. "If that's okay."

My mom beams at him. "Of course it's okay."

I can't believe how quickly my family has accepted Jackson into our lives. My parents and Grammy are hardly unfriendly people, but still, they've known him for three days and my mom's already okay with living in the same house as him for three weeks—okay with *me* living in the same house as him.

Not that I'm complaining. Three extra weeks in the same state as my soon-to-be long-distance boyfriend sounds like a dream. But—

"What about work?"

Jackson crosses the room and settles into his chair by my bed. He rests his elbows on the mattress and looks up at me.

"My contract doesn't start until September. I could stay." He swallows, his expression suddenly unsure. "If you want me to, that is."

"Of course I want you to!" I laugh and immediately regret it when a sharp pain stabs my midsection. "Oof." I grimace. "Although apparently how happy you make me is detrimental to my health."

Jackson smiles and presses a kiss to my hand. "I'll try to tone it down, then."

I won't make the mistake of laughing again, no matter how much I want to, but I feel the joy shining from my eyes. "Don't you dare."

Chapter Thirty-Three

Taylor

George and Pamela are at their house to help us settle in after I'm released from the hospital, showing us what rooms to use and where they keep extra towels and toilet paper. Mom and Pamela become fast friends as they talk about horses and owning a business. In the evening, Mom takes Pamela and George out to dinner to thank them before they need to drive back to B&B.

That leaves Jackson and me alone and without interruption for the first time since our last painful conversation at our spot by Libby Creek at the ranch.

Now that I'm mostly upright and no longer have tubes up my nose or an IV poking into my arm, I'm dying to kiss my boyfriend again. Fortunately, he's on the same wavelength, holding me on his lap on the couch and kissing me softly while gently trying to keep from jostling my stitches.

While having Jackson's heart is the ultimate prize, I'm definitely putting kissing down in the "appreciated perks" column.

We develop a routine after that. Time passes faster and more painfully than I thought possible. I'm under strict instructions to walk every day, starting with ten-minute struggles to the end of George and Pamela's driveway and building up to a slow stroll around the block.

The three of us play cards and watch TV to pass the time. My mom—bless her—disappears for long stretches of the day when she knows I won't need her. She has full use of Jackson's truck and says she wants to see some of the sights in the area.

One afternoon a few days after my release from the hospital, my mom is out exploring the Buffalo Bill Center of the West museums while Jackson and I play a lazy game of gin rummy on the couch as I recover from my morning walk, a tray set on the cushion between us for a table.

"Your turn," Jackson nudges me.

I blink and absently pick up the card that's upturned on the top of the discard pile. I'm zoned out thinking about the last week and a half.

"Are you going to reschedule your hike to Gannett Peak?" I ask Jackson.

I feel simultaneously guilt-ridden and cherished that Jackson gave up his trip because of my injury. With how much he'd been looking forward to it, I'd hate for him to miss out altogether.

He shrugs noncommittally, eyes trained on his hand of cards. "Maybe." He pulls a card out of his hand to discard, picking up a new one.

"You should," I press.

Jackson lifts his eyes to mine. "I want to. Financially though, this next year is going to be tighter than I'd anticipated."

His dad. The stolen money. "Oh," I manage. I drop my eyes to my cards and sort the matches.

Jackson has been open with me about his realizations about how his dad's actions—both now and when his mom got sick—distorted his own views of love and family. Still, though, I don't want to push him to share more than he's comfortable with.

"I was going to buy a house," Jackson says. I look up again in surprise. "With the money in the trust. It was supposed to be my down payment. I wanted to create a place for myself that would feel like home."

He shrugs again. "I don't think I had felt that since my mom passed away."

My nose burns as I blink back tears. I've never met Jackson's father—and Jackson tells me I never will, if he has anything to say about it—but this may be the closest I've ever come to hating another person.

I set my cards face down on my lap and reach across the game to take Jackson's hand in mine. "You'll get the money back, I'm sure of it. And then you can buy your house and find that home feeling again."

Jackson chuckles and squeezes my hand. "I already did, though. Without buying a house."

I tilt my head in a silent question.

"Whenever I'm with you, it feels like home."

Part of me wants to roll my eyes, even as I fight a giddy smile. The sincerity and love on Jackson's face tell me that his words are not a line, they're the truth, and I fall even more in love with him for it.

Our game of gin rummy gets pushed aside as we turn our attention toward a . . . sweeter activity.

We have gotten very good at kissing.

AFTER A WEEK, THE walking and talking and kissing gives me an idea.

"I want to visit Artist Point again before I leave Wyoming," I tell Jackson.

I'm sure I can do it as I gain more strength and the pain in my abdomen lessens to a dull ache. Artist Point has its own parking lot, and the outlook is a shorter walk from there than the turns around the block I'm supposed to be working up to.

It's a long car ride to Yellowstone from here, and the short drives I've taken to my doctor's appointments have been painful, but once I'm cleared for a flight across the country, surely a drive up to Artist Point won't be a problem.

Jackson and my mom are supportive of my plan, but cautious. At my next appointment, Mom asks the doctor—a Dr. Cartwright now, not Dr. Freeman anymore since I've been discharged—what he thinks.

"It won't be easy," he warns. "But having a specific goal to work toward can only help. Taylor will be more motivated to keep up with her daily walks and other exercises if there's a purpose behind it all." He looks at me. "Don't overdo it, though. And your daily deep breathing with the spirometer will be critical if you want to make it through even a short walk in those higher altitudes."

I'm a model patient after that, never missing my walk and faithfully checking off the list of home exercises from the physical therapist.

Finally, at a Friday appointment three weeks after I was discharged from the hospital, the doctor declares me "fit to fly."

SATURDAY MORNING, THE THREE of us load into Jackson's truck—me in the back seat with extra pillows—and Jackson drives us slowly up the mountain to Yellowstone.

Every bump in the road makes me wince, and Jackson notices. Every time I look up, I see the reflection of his eyes in the rearview mirror, watching me instead of the road.

"Are you sure you're up for this?" he asks.

"Yes. The doctor said it would be uncomfortable, but the plane ride tomorrow will be, too." I shake my head. "Who knows when I'll be back in Wyoming. I want to see Artist Point one more time before I leave."

Begrudgingly, Jackson keeps driving, and soon we're passing through the gate into Yellowstone. After my weeks of recovery, the trees and river are a welcome sight. I wish we had the time, and I had the energy, to show my mom more of Yellowstone's natural wonders, but Artist Point is ambitious enough for one day.

We pull into the Artist Point parking lot early enough that spots close to the sidewalk are easy to find. The air is still cool, and I'm glad to have my flannel-lined jacket, even if it looks a little silly paired with the baggy sweatpants that give my sore stomach the space it needs to heal.

I gingerly slide out of the truck with my mom's help and make it to the sidewalk. I hold my hand to my abdomen to brace myself and slowly start down the paved path to the overlook. Jackson hovers on one side of me, his hand on my arm. My mom brackets my other side.

It's a Saturday in August, so we knew Artist Point would be busy today, but we hoped that getting here early would mean we would be in and out before the area grows too congested. So far, so good. We're certainly not the only people here, but the crowds are thin. With my sentinels standing guard on either side, it's unlikely anyone will bump into me.

Finally, we reach the upper overlook, and it's a beautiful view. The last time we were here, though, Jackson and I had our *moment* at the secondary overlook that's up a set of wide, cement stairs.

Jackson notices my focus on the stairwell and shakes his head like he's reading my mind. "I don't think that's a good idea."

I've been navigating the staircase at George and Pamela's house for about a week now, but this one is taller and steeper.

"I think I can do it," I tell him. "I want to."

His disapproving expression doesn't waver.

"I'll stop and turn around if it pulls too much. Or if I get tired." I tilt my head to smile at Jackson. "Please?"

Jackson sighs. "Fine. I'll stay behind you."

My mom chuckles. "I'll wait here. But be careful, please."

I take the stairs one at a time, moving to the next step only after both feet have had time to settle on the previous. Jackson's behind me, his arms floating between us like he's ready to catch me at any moment. I know he would.

I'll admit that the journey up the stairs is slower and more tiring than I anticipated, but when we reach the top, it's well worthwhile.

Not only for the view, but also for the feeling of satisfaction that rushes through my chest at the accomplishment. This was hard, and I did it.

It makes me think I can do other hard things, too. I can keep my relationship with Jackson strong during our time apart. I can learn all the ins and outs of Steed Farm so that when my parents are ready to retire, they can pass the reins to me. I can go on more adventures like this amazing summer in Wyoming.

There's a low stone bench on one side of the overlook. I carefully sit down and enjoy the view as I rest. Jackson sits next to me, pulling me closer with an arm around my shoulder.

I lay my head against him and take a deep, happy breath.

Lowering his mouth to my ear, Jackson says in a low voice, "Mettlesome."

"What?" I lift my head to look at him, my forehead wrinkled.

He smiles. "My adjective for you. That's it: mettlesome."

This explanation doesn't clear things up. "Meddlesome? Like I meddle in other people's business?"

Jackson's smile flips into a frown. "No, that's Nick. You're mettlesome with two *T*s. Like full of mettle. Spirited. Like a mettlesome horse."

"Mettlesome," I repeat, letting the word roll around on my tongue. It makes me think of a strong, fine horse full of energy and ready to conquer the world. "I like it." I lean my head back against his shoulder. "I accept."

He chuckles, and I feel the low vibration as it spreads across his chest. "Have I told you lately how much I love you?"

I smile. "Not lately enough."

He kisses the side of my head. "Well, I do. I always knew I would meet the love of my life one day, but I didn't know it would be you. Now. I wasn't expecting that."

I blink away the tears in my eyes. I hadn't expected Jackson either, but he's been the best surprise.

"Disappointed?" I tease with a wobbly smile.

Jackson's expression remains earnest. He shakes his head back and forth. "Humbled. I know I'll never deserve you, but I promise I won't stop trying."

"Same," I whisper before he captures my lips in a searing kiss that's less careful than all the ones we've shared so far.

Maybe he figures that if I can climb a staircase, I can also withstand his fervid kisses. Or maybe he realizes that this may be the last private moment we have together before I get on a plane tomorrow and fly thousands of miles away from him.

Either way, as Jackson's hands cup either side of my face, his fingertips tangled in my hair and his mouth working seamlessly with mine, I can't help but think that this is the kiss I hoped for back in June the last time we were here together at Artist Point.

If I had gotten it then, maybe our story would have been simpler, but it wouldn't have been *us*. Despite the detours and hurt, our relationship has unfolded exactly how it needed to. It's true that neither of us is perfect, and we don't need to be because we *are* perfect for each other.

Epilogue

Eight Months Later

WALKING OUT OF MY supervisor's office, I text Taylor to see if she's available for a video call later tonight. I didn't want to get her hopes up before everything was settled, but I figure it's close enough to settled now, and besides, I can't wait any longer to share the news.

A few minutes later, my phone buzzes with her response: five exclamation marks. I'm taking it as a yes.

I leave work and drive west toward the mountains—and my apartment in north Boulder.

For the last eight months, I've felt like I'm missing a chunk of my heart in everything that I do. It sounds stupid, but I swear the sun is not as sunny without Taylor. We talk on the phone or video call every night, and we text constantly, but it's not the same as having her in my arms.

I visited her in Florida over Christmas, mostly because she has family there for us to spend the holiday with, and I don't have *any* family I want to spend the holidays with. It was also a little because I was worried about her traveling after she told me that the pressure from the seat belt in the car was still making the area around her incision site uncomfortable. I didn't want her sitting with that pressure for five hours or more on a plane.

Taylor's flight home after her surgery was rough on her, and I think I was overly sensitive about her getting on a plane again.

The drive to my apartment is only a few minutes. Soon enough, I'm pulling into the parking lot at my apartment complex. It's one of those large commercial places that cram as many units as possible into the square footage. I've lived in my one-bedroom apartment here ever since I graduated from college and could afford a place without roommates.

I've always liked having my own space, but lately it's felt lonely and too quiet.

The apartment is not anything I'll miss.

The mountains . . . probably. Okay, definitely. But not as much as I miss Taylor now.

She says the hardest struggle for her since her injury is not being able to ride.

Considering *how* Taylor got injured, I wouldn't mind if she never rode a horse again in her life, but then she'd be miserable, missing out on one of the activities she loves most. It also wouldn't be practical because her job is literally to ride and train horses.

She was only cleared to ride again without restrictions two months ago, and from what she tells me, she's determined to make up for lost time.

After I change into more comfortable clothes, I sort through my mail. With some uneasiness, I rip open an envelope labeled with my lawyer's return address, but it's only my most recent billing statement.

Back in October, I filed a civil suit against my father in an attempt to have the money from my trust returned. The money's gone, of course. I learned that he's been skimming money from the account for years now. The return on "investment" my dad imagined he'd be receiving from this last scheme predictably never came to fruition, and he doesn't have enough money to pay me back on his own.

Unbelievably, he can't understand what he did wrong or why I would sue him. He'd been laying the guilt on thick until I finally took my lawyer's advice and blocked him.

The lawsuit hasn't been settled yet—and may not be for a long time—but I hope he can come up with the money before it is. Despite everything, he's still my dad, and I don't want the court to decide to levy his bank accounts or garnish his wages on my behalf if it can be prevented.

It is what it is. I've always hated that phrase, but I appreciate it now for how simply it expresses my reluctant acceptance of circumstances I can't change.

When the anger and grief start to overwhelm me, I take a page from my wise girlfriend's book and find something beautiful to look at instead. Taylor's photo on the lock screen of my phone has come in handy many times.

Meanwhile, though, I'm spending my savings on lawyer fees. The new twelve-month engineering contract I signed yesterday is well-timed for several reasons.

I cook myself a simple dinner and check the time. It's seven here, making it nine at Taylor's house—she'll start fading within the hour.

Time to call her and share my news.

As soon as her face appears on the screen, everything in me settles. "Hey, beautiful."

She's sitting up in bed, bookshelves in the background. I catch sight of the stuffed bison I bought her while she was in the hospital, and it makes me smile.

She grins. "Hi, cowboy."

Because I'm the furthest thing from a cowboy—which I proved quite thoroughly when I tried to help her at the farm when I was there for Christmas—she thinks this nickname is hilarious.

I almost roll my eyes, but she follows up the teasing with the same thing she tells me every night when we talk. "I miss you."

"I miss you, too. We'll see each other soon, though."

She sighs. "Yeah. Should I plan a trip to Colorado this summer, do you think? I could come out before you leave for Gannett Peak in July."

I rescheduled my Gannett Peak hike to this summer. The earlier timing means it won't be as icy, which is a bummer, but it also means the hike in and out will be easier—at least over land.

I struggle to hold back my grin a little longer. "You can come to Colorado this summer, but I won't be here."

Taylor's forehead crinkles adorably. "What?"

"You know how this is the last month of my current contract? Well, I signed a new one yesterday."

This information clears nothing up for Taylor—not that I intended it to—and her eyes narrow. "Okay?"

Finally, I smile and share the news. "I signed a contract with a new company. In Florida. Ocala, actually."

Taylor stills, so much so that I start to think the video call is frozen from a bad connection.

Finally, my words seem to register. "You can't move to Florida!" she practically shouts.

Well, that's not quite the reaction I expected.

Now it's my turn to be confused. "I thought you'd be excited. I thought we both want to be done with long distance."

She sets her hand on her hips. "Of course I want to be with you, dummy. But there are no mountains in Florida! The day we met you told me that mountains are one of the two loves of your life. How can you live somewhere where there are no mountains?"

I laugh, shaking my head, because this concern is easy to address. "Taylor, the only love of my life is *you*. I'll be anywhere so long as it's with you." I shrug. "Besides, the Appalachians aren't too far away. They'll make for some nice weekend trips."

Even through the phone screen, I can tell her eyes are welling up. "Are you sure?"

"Yes," I say confidently. "I'm tired of only seeing you through a screen. I want to be able to hug you every day and deliver more of those kisses I promised you. I'm done wasting time I could be spending in your arms. This is the easiest decision I've ever made."

Taylor sniffles. "In that case . . ." A beautiful huge smile overtakes her face. "When do you move?"

I laugh. "The beginning of May."

"Oh my gosh! I can see you every day, and we can eat dinner together, and you can play cards with me and Grammy, and we can drive to the beach, and . . ." She trails off as a blush spreads across her face.

"And what?" I press, though her pink cheeks give me a pretty good idea of what she was going to say.

I can see her eyes spark even through the phone screen. She tosses her hair. "And I can kiss you any time I want."

Smirking, I tease, "Any man in his right mind would move across the country for that promise alone."

We talk for a few minutes longer—making plans for my move and our relationship now that we'll be living in the same place—and I think about how quickly life can change.

There was a day when I was fifteen when I was a normal high schooler. Then, the next day, I was a kid whose mom had cancer and whose dad was moving out.

When I was a senior in high school, there was a day when I had a mother. Then, the next day, I didn't anymore.

When I was packing to drive to B&B Ranch last summer, if someone had tried to tell me that in a year, I'd be so in love that I'd change jobs and move to Florida to be with my girlfriend, I'm certain I would have laughed in their face. That wasn't me.

But today, it is me. And I can't wait to see what joys tomorrow will bring.

Bonus Epilogue

To read a scene from Jackson and Taylor's future, download the bonus epilogue!

https://BookHip.com/MAKMXPV

Or visit **www.juliemilo.com** and sign up for my newsletter!

Acknowledgements

In the summer of 2025, my family and I took a vacation that inspired us all. We stayed at an all-inclusive guest ranch outside of Cody, Wyoming, much like the one depicted in *Artist Point.*

I was in awe of the natural beauty of the area, including in Yellowstone National Park. It was truly the experience of a lifetime, and I wanted to capture the spectacular, expansive feeling of it all in writing. I hope I've accomplished that in this book.

Though *Artist Point* is Jackson and Taylor's love story, it's also a love letter to Wyoming and Yellowstone National Park. I hope that the experiences and landscapes I describe inspire you to one day visit Yellowstone to see and do it all for yourself. God's creation is astounding.

Thank you to my beta readers: Rebekah Goodman for her general feedback; Sharon Miner, author of the *Beloved Horses* series, for her equestrian expertise; Cassandra Joelle for her knowledge of Cody and the surrounding area; and Megan Fallon for her verification of my use of climbing gear, locations, and details.

That said, any errors in the details about horses, Wyoming, or climbing are my own.

Special thank you to Jenny for giving me feedback on the first fifty pages of this manuscript. And to Jenny and Melanie and the rest of the "Well Women" for their support and comments.

Thank you Sydney Christensen of Sydney Christensen Creations. I wanted the cover of *Artist Point* the book to show Artist Point the location. I gave her some photographs I took of the view from Artist Point and asked her to make it look like a painting. The end result is stunning.

Thank you to my tireless book coach and editor, Ruth Shilling (www.rseditorial.co). Writing this book was not smooth sailing; I think I edited it more than any of my other books so far. Plus, the short timeline I had in mind meant we had to turn around the edits quickly. Thank you, Ruth, for working with me on my ambitious self-imposed deadline, and for loving Jackson and Taylor.

Thank you to Alicia Whitaker (@aliciasalwaysreading on Instagram) for her eagle-eyed proofreading. Knowing that Alicia is going to check all my commas and hyphens means I can focus on the words, the story, and the characters.

Thank you to my children, Gabriel and Ana. Stories from our time together in Wyoming are peppered throughout this book, and Gabriel still asks me at least once a month when we can go back again.

As always, thank you to my husband Andy.

Finally, thank you readers! It's more fun to write stories knowing you're there to read them. If you've loved this, or any of my other books, consider leaving a review on Amazon, Goodreads, or another bookish platform. Reviews truly make a huge difference for authors, especially indie authors like me!

Also by Julie Milo

Delaneys in Love series

Love in the Stacks

Love in the Lab

Love at the Lake

Second Chance in Asheville

About the Author

Julie Milo spends most of her time reading and writing. When she's not reading and writing scholarly stuff for her day job, she's reading romance, nonfiction, and literary fiction for fun. She writes closed door/kisses only (also called "sweet") romances.

Julie was raised, but not born, in Florida where she started dictating stories to her parents before she even knew how to write. By kindergarten she was writing and illustrating picture books and subjecting her classmates to read alouds at school. While the illustrating did not stick (her drawing skills never evolved past about third grade), the writing did, and for most of her childhood, her answer to "What do you want to be when you grow up?" was "an author." Returning to writing decades later is a dream come true, and Julie is proud to finally be able to call herself an author.

Julie currently lives on the Gulf coast of Florida with her thoughtful husband, two amazing children, and two dogs (one delightful pit bull and one very energetic black lab). She loves dessert and hates cold weather.

You can learn more about Julie and her books at www.juliemilo.com.

Made in the USA
Coppell, TX
25 June 2026

83148535R00146